I0716120

CORRUPTION

NEON
BOOK TWO

ALLYSON LINDT

ACELETTE PRESS

For everyone who knows what lengths they'd go to for those they love

CHAPTER 1
DAHLIA

Would I ever reach the point where I could sit in front of two ancient gods and give them a look that said their opinion was irrelevant?

And mean it?

"I'd like to speak to my niece—my sister—alone." Urd looked like a statue carved of alabaster, in the way she held herself, the dim light of the bar's back room reflecting off her skin, and the deep stare she focused on Fenrir and Freyr.

Fen shifted his body to half-block mine in the doorway to the back room. He and Frey owned a burlesque club that was old school meets high tech—dark, hand-carved furniture and neon lights—and tonight was my debut as their headlining dancer.

My name on their marquee was supposed to attract the attention of the gods. Those who had a price on my head, not the second of two surviving dragons who were as old as dirt. Literally, as far as I could tell.

"It's up to Dahlia to decide if she wants to talk to you," Freyr said.

Yup, that was me—the woman related to two dragons. To be fair, Urd and her actual sisters supposedly had thousands of relatives running around in the world with no idea they were descended from dragons. I was the first one who had ever manifested any sign of my ancestry.

Like, in all of history. There hadn't been another new dragon between when they popped into existence and now.

I wanted to tell Urd to go fuck herself. That she didn't have a right to call me niece or sister, given that she didn't care I existed until I started to grow scales. I'd told a number of gods off in the past—it was why there was a price on my head—but honestly, she terrified me.

"I won't speak to you alone." I forced my voice to remain steady. I was shit at hiding my emotion most of the time, much to the dismay of the people who raised and trained me as an assassin, but I knew how to fake *I don't give a shit how powerful you are*. "However, I will speak with you."

Settling into the seat next to Frey, I composed myself as well as one could while wearing nothing but pasties, ruffled panties, and a silky bathrobe and staring down a dragon in human form.

Fen pulled up another chair, flipped the back toward Urd, and straddled it. He rested his arms on the back and fixed a glare on her. Though his wolf was tucked away, the challenge of a predator flashed in his eyes, and a low, threatening growl rolled from his chest.

My relationship with these men was complicated. They'd become more to me than the gods I went to for sex or protection. I couldn't imagine my life without them. But I didn't have the kind of love for them that they had for each other.

I'd never met Urd before, but she and her sisters were responsible for a series of prophecies that had turned gods against gods, and trapped humans in the crossfire, both intentionally and otherwise. I had been one of those humans, plucked from the foster care system in my pre-teens, and trained to lie, spy, and kill, based on Urd's prophecies.

She wasn't one of the gods involved in my upbringing, but as far as I was concerned, she put the visions out there, for the world to do with as they would, and stepped away to let it happen, so she was as guilty as the gods who tried to mold me.

Was there some resentment on my part toward most gods?

Only an overwhelming amount.

"This bravado and protectiveness is charming."

Urd's smile was as cool as the pearlescent sheen on her skin. "I'm not here to hurt you."

"But it's unlikely you would stop someone else from doing so, either," I said.

She nodded. "That's a fair assumption on your part. However, it's also one of the reasons I'm here."

"To stop someone else from hurting me?" I could make a joke about dangling modifiers, but she didn't look like she had a sense of humor. "I'm good on that front. Thanks." With Fen and Frey by my side, I was pretty safe.

The fact that I could shift into a dragon should help, but I hadn't learned how to control that yet.

Urd sighed heavily. "I'm here at least in part to apologize for not being present in the past. I understand how you feel about the way my prophecies and name—"

"You couldn't possibly."

She raised an eyebrow at my interruption. "—and I know I need to step up and take control of the situation."

"So you've disbanded the Followers of Urd?" Frey asked.

She shook her head. "We all know you don't disband an organization of fanatics; they find their own path if you don't give them one. I have presented myself as Urd, though. I've taken the reins. And I'd like the three of you—especially you, Dahlia—to join me."

"I'm not much of a joiner." That was part lie. I'd spent a large part of my life looking for a place where I felt like I belonged. Kept hoping it would be the campus I was raised on, or at least among the people I grew up with. These days, I knew that my best friend, Magnus, was more of a sister than the dragons would ever be. And while Frey and Fen had a love that knew no time or boundaries, I had the two of them looking out for me.

"We'll fight to keep innocent people alive, but we won't take sides in this ridiculous, manufactured war," Frey said.

There were two factions, the Followers of Urd and The Order of Mistletoe—the group that had raised me—but they both seemed to pursue similar objectives. The only beings who mattered to either side were those who could help them shape the future to their benefit. "You know that, even if you stepped up to lead, FU is still killing gods, right?"

"I wish you wouldn't call it that." Urd winced. "That is one of the things I hope to correct. I don't want anyone killing in my name or because of our prophecies."

"It's a little late for that." It wasn't that I wanted to be difficult just because. I'd seen so many die in this fight, all for the egos of a few gods who couldn't accept they might not be immortal. Even worse, everyone treated the prophecies like they were set in stone, including the dragons who had written them.

I'd learned recently that wasn't the case. The visions Urd and her sisters had were possibilities but not always a given, and if people understood that, it was possible fewer would be killed.

"Please, give me a chance to prove things will change," Urd said.

I shook my head. "I don't know why you need me to be a part of that."

"I don't. But you are one of us, and I'd rather work with you than without you."

Funny, how that didn't matter until I gained access to my own powers and visions. How the dragon bloodline still didn't matter to the thousands of others like me—with a dragon as a parent—who had been abandoned over the centuries. I clucked and shook my head. "I'm going to have to say no. Good luck, though. Don't forget to write." I furrowed my brow. "On second thought, don't write anything down. Pretty sure that was what started this mess in the first place."

In a blink, Urd's cool expression vanished. Heat surged through the room, and a soft growl cut the air. The afterimage of a dragon flashed in front of her, obscuring her human form.

And like that, the terrifying display was gone again.

My heart hammered against my ribs, as Urd stood. She gave us a short bow. "Please do reach out if you change your mind."

She disappeared from the room, something no one should be able to do without Frey removing the magic that kept NEON hidden from most of the outside world.

On some level, I registered that Urd hadn't left a way to get a hold of her, but overall, it didn't matter. Her quick *did I really just see that* intimidation tactic had worked, reminding me I might be a dragon but I was still barely thirty, compared to her who-even-knew-how-old.

If I pissed her off enough, would she crush me and hope the next dragon who emerged was easier to deal with? I didn't want the thought to scare me, but it did.

CHAPTER 2
FENRIR

When Urd let her rage slip, it took all of my self-control to not react in kind, let my wolf out, and lunge for her throat.

I wouldn't attack her for her very wrong opinions about warring gods, but to come into our place of business—our home—and imply the kind of threat she had called for retaliation. Frey's presence was the reason I kept myself in check. Centuries ago, I almost lost myself to the beast inside. These days, I stayed away from battle because Frey saved me from the edge of insanity back then.

Over time, I'd met a lot of people who wondered what a god of war—*I*—had in common with a god of sex—Freyr.

The answer was *passion*. Sex was a lot closer to fighting than most realized, and I knew one way to burn off this clawing sensation that didn't involve battle.

Based on the scents after Urd vanished and the sound of racing pulses and quickened breathing, I wasn't the only one who needed an outlet. I didn't have the patience to vocalize it, though. When I turned to Dahlia, she stared back with defiance.

Even when she had been mortal, she wore that look. She refused to cower in the face of any god, and that was one of my favorite things about her.

I pushed away from my chair, not caring that it clattered to the ground, and dragged my nose up the side of her neck with a growl that was meant to entice, rather than terrorize.

She tilted her head, exposing more skin, and let the sides of her robe fall open. And then she did something brand new for her and held up her index finger as it shifted from human flesh to a single dragon claw. She cut a clean line down my chest that healed almost as quickly as it appeared but left the sting of pain.

My wolf didn't know the difference between Dahlia's dragon and Urd's, but I did, and the mix of *friend* and *foe* raised my lust to a whole new level. "Are you trying to provoke me, Duckie?"

"There is no *try*. There is only *do* or *do not*."

I'd take that as a *yes*.

Frey would join in as he wished, but right now I wanted Dahlia. The woman who could've been destroyed by half a dozen gods in the first quarter-century of her life, but still looked immortals in the eye and refused to flinch.

I wrapped a hand around her throat and raised her to her feet. Her pulse hammered against the fleshy bit of my palm, her whimper hummed along my skin, and I felt it when she swallowed. But she never blinked.

"So. Fucking. Delicious." I was done talking or thinking. I crushed my mouth to hers.

In a blink, Frey was behind her. A sharp *snick* cracked in the air when he pulled the belt from her robe in a single, fluid motion. I pushed the covering off her arms, and he bound her wrists behind her back with the silk belt.

Dahlia's gasp was delight mixed with fear and defiance, but this wasn't the same kind of terror that Urd tried to evoke. This was high-strung anticipation for what came next.

I licked a line up her neck to bite her earlobe, and relished her groan. Next, I caught her pasties in my teeth, one at a time, and spit them aside. I wanted to taste so much of her. To lick away the sweat that mingled with body glitter from the dancing she'd done earlier. To sink my teeth into her skin until she cried out, then bury my face between her legs until she screamed.

And I couldn't find the words for any of that. I was lost in the scents of her arousal and Frey's. I tore away her panties, leaving a whisper of red on her hips that vanished as she healed.

"*Fuck her,*" I growled.

Frey smirked. He was calm and in control and infuriatingly sexy.

Hunger coursed through my veins as I watched him slip his fingers between Dahlia's legs, then inside her. Her chest heaved with every breath, as she pressed back into his touch, unable to do much more while she was restrained.

Frey pumped inside Dahlia until she was grinding against him, her breath coming in short pants. He pulled out and pressed his fingers to my mouth, and I devoured her taste and her juices.

After dragging down his zipper, Frey freed his cock, sat, and guided Dahlia back into his lap. Her eyelids fluttered and her lips parted in a silent gasp when he penetrated her.

I watched the display with hungry fascination, as Frey spread his legs and Dahlia's wide, putting her gorgeous pussy on display with him buried deep inside her.

Falling to my knees at their feet, I scraped my lips along the inside of her bare thigh.

The sounds that tore from her throat spurred me higher. Closer to her core. I dragged my tongue over both of them, licking along Frey's skin and lapping at Dahlia's juices. A few tastes weren't enough. I buried my face between their legs, devouring the sounds they made, as greedily as I drank in the flavor.

When I moved my mouth to wrap around Dahlia's clit, she arched away from Frey's touch and struggled against my tongue. She writhed as I traced runes around her swollen nub. I sucked hard, loving the feeling of her grinding into my face.

When Dahlia came, it was with a string of, "*Oh fuck, oh fuck, oh fuck. Fuck me,*" that rang in my ears. I didn't pull away until she sank into Frey, her body mostly limp.

I raised my face, and with one finger under her chin, forced her gaze to mine. She stared back with a tiny smile.

"My turn." My voice was gravel, and forming the words took effort I'd rather be using for something else.

Dahlia nodded.

When I stood, my dick strained against my jeans in protest at being caged. As I tugged down my zipper, some of the pressure was released, but not enough. Wrapping my hand around my shaft was both a relief and a promise of what came next.

Dahlia's moan when I knotted my fingers in her hair was tasty. I lowered her head to my cock, and she took me into her mouth without hesitation. *Fuuuck* her lips felt incredible wrapped around me. Especially when Frey made her whimper as she rode him, and the hum vibrated through my skin.

I jerked myself while she licked and sucked. She was a gorgeous creature, especially now, with her skin flushed and her scent alone enough to seduce me. I knew when Frey drew another orgasm from her by the way she paused in sucking me off. The ecstasy that washed across her face.

And I knew when he came as well, slamming inside her hard and fast, his grunts growing louder. More punctuated.

The entire symphony combined to push over the edge. I slipped from Dahlia's mouth as climax ripped through me, covering her face and chest with cum.

While she was still panting, trying to catch her breath, I dropped to my knees in front of her. Licking her clean seemed like the perfect conclusion to this intensity. Frey untied her and his cock slipped out of her, as I glided my tongue along her skin.

She tangled her fingers in my hair, holding me close while I licked along her chest. Her breasts. Her pussy again. Tasting myself. Her. Frey. Everything.

As need finally ebbed, the three of us moved to someplace more comfortable. Someplace where we could collapse together in a pile of warmth, and rest.

For now, the beast inside me was sated.

Days later, Urd's visit lingered in my thoughts while my wolf paced around it with discontent. With

Dahlia's fidgeting and Frey's snapping at little things, it was clear I wasn't the only one the encounter didn't sit well with. Fucking provided a distraction, but it wasn't sating what sat at my core.

The solution was to get away and help Dahlia with her training at the same time. I could teach her some control techniques, but I didn't know how to fly and she needed to master that as well. So we invited Magnus, who had been a Valkyrie for barely longer than Dahlia had been a dragon, and had mastered flight in that time.

The cabin we escaped to was in Norway, tucked away from everything. Frey teleported us from NEON to pick up Magnus, and then to our final destination. When we landed in the middle of the forest, the stale scent of death and gunpowder greeted me, bringing back memories of the last time I was here.

My teeth elongated without my permission, piercing my cheek before I forced them to retract.

"We should go someplace else." Frey's voice was even and calm.

"Is this where…" Magnus trailed off.

I nodded as I focused on filing my more primal reactions into nice, neat little drawers in my mind. "TOM sent Starkad to me, hoping I'd kill him." Starkad was a berserker, a warrior created distinctly for battle who could embody the spirit of a wolf. He wasn't the same kind of wolf I was, and he wasn't meant to have control when he was in his other form.

I took issue with some of the battles he'd chosen to fight, and I'd been here losing myself in the wilderness. Their hope had been that putting him in my path would lead to his destruction.

We were tentative allies now, instead, but the remnants of the firefight that ensued when I didn't destroy him—memories of the way TOM hunted us —hung in the air and in my memories.

"I refuse to let them soil one of the few remaining places I can find peace," I said.

We were taking a risk, coming here. Going anywhere out in the open, really. The organization that raised Dahlia was still hunting her, using technology she created to trace magical signatures. But Frey had the ability to mask places and people and take them off the grid. Make those spots invisible to the magical eye. While we were here, we should be hidden.

"So what now?" Magnus asked.

Always impatient. Always anxious to *go now*.

I didn't blame her. "Dahlia, would you rather do this humanoid or in your full form?" I knew the answer.

Wings appeared on her back, their span twice as long as her body, and sunlight glinting off the irides-cent purple and black. The same colors appeared on her arms and face, covering her in scales, and a tail grew from her very lower back, swishing lazily, wrapping around her ankles before flicking again.

Other than that, she was physically human. It was both adorable and sexy, that this was the form she preferred to shift to.

Magnus summoned wings as well, though hers were auburn and feathered, more like angel wings. "The part where your feet leave the ground is magic; it has nothing to do with the wings themselves." She floated half a meter above the dirt. "But the wings make steering and fighting easier."

She beat her wings and kicked up flurries of debris in the wind, then shot straight up and evened out, darting and weaving through the sky above the treetops.

Now we were having fun. I let my wolf form out. When I took my natural size and shape, I was about as large as a truck. I needed to run, so I chased Magnus, using tree trunks to bound higher and nip at her ankles before landing deftly on my feet again.

We circled back to the clearing, to find Frey lounged against a nearby tree, looking nonplussed.

Dahlia was scowling, though. Interesting effect, through the scales that covered her face. "Hello. Noob needing help." Frustration undercut her words.

I lay next to Frey's feet, to wait for the next round of play. My wolf wasn't in control, but I was comfortable letting the lines blur between it and me.

Magnus touched down lightly next to Dahlia. "There's not a lot to the first step," Magnus said. "You think *fly*, and you fly."

Dahlia closed her eyes. Seconds ticked away, and a frown crawled onto her face. More time passed, and she sighed heavily, looking at Magnus again. "Do I need to think of the happiest things? Any happy little thing? Did you forget a step? Do I need fairy dust?"

"I think you've already got the fairy dust." Magnus tweaked the tip of Dahlia's tail.

Dahlia jerked away, but her scowl was gone. "Okay. Think *fly*." Nothing happened. "*Fly*." She jumped and immediately landed on her feet. There was no lift. "*Fly*." She jumped again, pulled her knees to her chest, and fell on her ass.

I whimpered with sympathy. I could still talk, though it was more of a voice in their heads than my using my vocal cords, but this was the best I could come up with.

Dahlia moved to the nearest tree, climbed to the bottom branch, about two meters in the air, and jumped. The jarring of her hitting the ground was visible, and her frustration was tangible.

"This is bullshit." Dahlia pulled herself into the tree again. "I have wings. Dragons can fly. I want to fly." She moved up to the middle of the tree, closer to seven meters up.

"Don't do that." Frey's casual stance masked the tension running through his body.

"Too late." Dahlia perched on the edge of the branch. "I need a jump start is all. A fall that's a threat."

Frey clenched his jaw. "What happens if you fall and break something?"

"I heal really fast."

"Then falling isn't a threat for you," Frey said.

Dahlia shrugged.

Every muscle in my body tensed as I prepared to leap if I needed to catch her. I wanted what she was doing to work, but...

Dahlia squeezed her eyes shut tight and jumped.

CHAPTER 3
FREYR

My heart plummeted when Dahlia stepped off the tree branch, and the entire world slowed to a crawl. Without looking, I felt Fen tense, and Magnus was already in flight.

But Dahlia stopped a short distance above the ground and hovered in place, her eyes squeezed shut. She pried one eye open, then let out a loud *whoop*. "I'm floating. "

Magnus pulled up next to her and matched the hover. "You did it." The two radiated excitement.

Even Fen was wagging his tail.

"Next step, follow me." Magnus floated up higher.

Dahlia plummeted the rest of the way to the ground, kicking up a cloud of dust when she landed. Her scowl was back, etched more deeply into her face than ever. She climbed the tree again, moving easily with the proficiency of someone who'd been raised to get into and out of unusual spaces with minimal effort.

"You have to learn to fly without the tree," Magnus said.

Dahlia stuck her tongue out. "I'll do that after I learn to fly *with* the tree."

When she jumped, she didn't fall as far. But she couldn't rise higher either. For the next couple of hours, the frustration level swelled in the forest as she tried again and again to take flight, and never managed more than to hover a meter or two off the ground before plummeting to the dirt again.

About halfway through, Fen had given up and shifted back to his human form and joined me in holding up our tree as we watched. I doubted this was the short getaway he hoped for.

When Dahlia's responses came as much growl and bark as Fen's wolf, I'd had enough. "We should go."

"I'm going to get it." Dahlia spoke through clenched teeth.

Magnus looked frustrated as well. "You can fall on your ass anywhere. Besides, I want breakfast. Lunch?" She glanced at a wrist with no watch. "Whatever. I'm hungry."

"How do you do it?" Dahlia pushed to her feet and brushed the dust from her jeans. "How do you have this ability to run so far and fast, or fly, and willingly lock it away almost every day?"

I looked at Fen, knowing he had strong opinions on the matter.

He twisted his mouth. "It's the cost of living in a modern world. Would you give up your phone, computer, and internet connection forever, to fly when you wanted?"

"I might."

I knew better. "You wouldn't."

Dahlia puffed out her cheeks and exhaled noisily. "Fine, I wouldn't. Let's go eat."

"You pick where," I said to Dahlia. "And you drive." It would give her practice with a different skill, and hopefully restore a little of her confidence after the lackluster flying attempts.

She scrubbed her palms on her thighs several more times. "Okay." She held her hands out.

Magnus and I each grasped one and Frey took my hand. The forest vanished and a street in a small town appeared around us.

"Where did you decide?" I asked. It wasn't European—the architecture was too new, but the street layout wasn't quite American either.

Dahlia looked around with a faint frown.

"Australia," Magnus said. "Perth."

Fen raised an eyebrow and sniffed the air. "Fresh seafood?"

"And baked goods." There was a hint of doubt in Dahlia's reply.

"This is where—" Magnus bit the words off and gave Dahlia a questioning look.

Dahlia crammed her hands in her pockets and started walking. "It's where I landed before TOM caught me. There's a little shop around the corner with amazing food and I thought maybe now was a good time to thank the owner." The longer she spoke, the more confident her voice grew.

She hadn't meant to bring us here. Where did she intend to land instead?

It didn't seem like now was the time to push the issue. We could talk through it in a more intimate setting, to keep her from feeling defensive and see what kind of ideas we could come up with to help Dahlia figure this out. The stumbling block we'd all run into was her coming into powers we'd all had since the beginning of our existence.

Except Magnus, who seemed to fall—or rise—naturally into being a Valkyrie.

There were new gods out there, but none that I knew of who could shift or had wings. When we were back home, I'd put out a call and see if anyone of the new gods could teleport. Maybe they had some advice for her.

This was a disadvantage to having distanced ourselves from most other immortals, and allying ourselves with the few others who had done the same—being out of the loop meant not knowing who was out there now.

Min may have a good idea. I made a mental note to call him when we got home.

"What are you—" Dahlia's tone was panicked. She faltered in her step. "*No*."

"Dahlia?" I rested a hand on her arm.

She shook me off and looked past me with a gaze that said she wasn't here. "It can't— What?"

"She's seeing something, isn't she?" Magnus sounded concerned.

Fen stepped behind Dahlia and gripped her shoulders, holding her in place. She tried to jerk free, but he held her tight and backed up out of the flow of foot traffic.

Taking her hand again, I grasped her chin with my other hand and tried to get her to look at me. Her stare was still unfocused and though she was fighting, she wasn't responding to *us*.

"Dahlia." I made my tone firmer. "Where are you?"

She continued to mutter incomplete thoughts.

"*Dahlia*," I barked.

She turned to me, and seemed to sink against Fen's touch. "Oh, fuck me." She sounded drained.

"What did you see?" I assumed one of the visions of the future that came with being a dragon, but I was looking for details.

She shook her head. "I don't know. It didn't

make sense beyond a really bad feeling. As in, I felt like I was channeling... someone?" She pressed her palm to her forehead and leaned more weight against Fen. "Fuck me."

"Let's go home." I adjusted my hand to weave my fingers with hers instead of gripping tight.

Dahlia scrubbed her face and straightened up. "No. It's okay. I'm okay. I need to get used to these stupid glimpses of potential futures, right?"

I didn't know if that was the case or not. Maybe Urd and Artura had locked themselves away from the world partially because the visions were taxing. They didn't talk about it, or much of anything, so it was difficult to say. But Artura had offered to teach Dahlia some things. "We'll go get breakfast if you'll talk to Artura about the visions."

Dahlia worked her jaw, and I tried to anticipate what her argument would be.

"All right." She yielded.

She must be very out of sorts if she was giving up without a fight.

As we started walking again, the feeling of residual magic slid along my skin. It was faint, like the scent of pending rain on a spring day, which made it difficult for me to determine if it was a fresh signature or lingered from a being who was here days ago.

"I wondered if I'd ever see you again." The woman radiated kindness.

Dahlia's smile was warm, but to someone who knew her, it didn't mask the tension that kept her body coiled and on high alert. "I found my way home, thanks to you. But I wanted to do the trip right this time, so I brought my sister. My guys. They keep me out of trouble, you know." Her tone was light and chatty, bordering on rambling, as she introduced us to *Tania*.

Which tended to mean her mind was racing but she had to be *on* for whomever she was talking to.

"She's lying." I matched my playful tone to hers, and slid in just enough magic-tinged seduction to make Tania feel at ease. "We all get in more trouble together." I winked.

"Don't listen to him." Dahlia's laugh was bright and the right level of amused and nervous. At times like this, her training to be anyone the situation required shone through. "We're really harmless, especially as a group."

I fed a little more magical suggestion into the air, helping Tania believe the words. She'd remember us, but not as a threat, regardless of who asked. I had to push harder than normal, as the mystical essence in the air was more potent now. It wrapped around me in an uncomfortably tight embrace.

"I believe it." Tania grinned and pointed us toward a table. "Let me get you drinks, and you figure out what you'd like to eat."

I lightly touched her arm. "What do you recommend? Tell you what—you pick for us, and we'll take it to go."

"You're a brave lot. You've got it." Tania sounded amused and at ease.

"To go?" Dahlia asked softly after Tania walked away. "So I'm not the only one whose skin feels like it's going to crawl off."

"No," Magnus and Fen said in unison.

Most of the time I could forget I was surrounded by hunters, but at this moment I was grateful for it. I could fight, but I'd rather not, and having these three on my side made me feel better about any pending conflict.

Our conversation went dead while we waited for Tania to return with our food. The four of us were too busy watching our surroundings while trying to look like we were doing anything else.

Tania returned a few minutes later with two paper bags that looked ready to burst at the seams. "Here you go, all set."

"Thank you." I poured the warmth and charm into my voice. "For taking care of our girl." I pressed two large bills into her palm.

"Oh no, I can't. I did it because she needed help. No other reason." Tania flushed.

"Please." I pushed the godly charm a little harder. "We'd be lost without her and I'll be hurt if you don't. You wouldn't want that."

"Of course I wouldn't." Tania pocketed the money.

Fen nudged me hard in the back.

Maybe I was pushing a little too hard. Whatever was in the air was throwing me off. Fen took the food and we headed outside. I reached for people's hands.

"We shouldn't do this here." Dahlia shook her head. "I know, I've been here before, but if TOM is looking for magical signatures..."

"We should go back to where we arrived. Maybe retrace our steps. Make sure we don't send anyone looking for us directly to Tania's doorstep," Magnus said.

That made sense. The four of us retraced our path back to the spot Dahlia had ported us into, and the longer we walked, the more my uneasiness grew.

"Take Magnus back," Dahlia said. "I'll meet you at NEON."

"Duckie." Fen's tone was warning, and if he'd pulled out the nickname, he was trying to soften the blow.

She scowled. "I need to get this right. I need to get *something* right. I'll meet you back at NEON."

I didn't like this plan. It didn't matter, because Dahlia had already vanished.

I took Fen and Magnus, dropped Magnus off with a few old friends. She'd refused to go home recently if Dahlia wasn't there. I didn't blame her.

Within seconds, Fen and I were back at NEON.

Dahlia wasn't here. I'd feel her if she was in a different room. If she was anywhere within any of my spheres of protection. I'd be able to sense her if she was somewhere else in the world, and she'd just landed in the wrong place.

"What's wrong?" Fen asked.

"Dahlia's gone."

"Gone where?"

"Nowhere." It didn't matter how far I extended my senses, across the entire world, I couldn't find her aura.

CHAPTER 4

DAHLIA

When my new location came into view, I was in a building, but it wasn't NEON. My gut lurched before my brain caught up, and I summoned everything I'd learned so far to get me the fuck out of the current TOM training facility.

The problem was, I couldn't see the outside world. I must be doing something wrong, because my magic didn't think anything existed except this campus.

"On your knees." The shout came from behind me, and I found myself surrounded by half a dozen TOM soldiers leveling assault rifles at me.

Instinct said to follow the barked order. Years of training that insisted I comply in an impossible situation until I had a way out.

Recent events reminded me I was a dragon and who the fuck did they think they were?

A dragon who didn't know how to use her own power and who was facing off against a group of people with bullets that could kill some immortals. I wasn't ready to be their dragon test subject.

"*Now.*"

I hid a jump at the barked order

"Dahlia." Vidar's smooth tone made my knees shake more than a room full of guns pointed at my head.

But I'd learned from a young age to never back down, even from a god. He'd been the god to teach me that. "Hello, Vidar."

"Nice of you to visit. To what do we owe this pleasure?"

"I wanted to see the new place. See if you really made it nearly identical to the old one." The campus I was raised on had been raised when the ancient god sealed underneath was released, but Vidar had brought most of the surviving members of TOM to a new location that closely resembled the old one.

Vidar made a wide sweeping gesture. "What do you think?"

Were we going to talk about the fact that he'd kidnapped me and had a trusted friend invade my dreams and torture me, to get information I didn't know I had?

"Just like coming home." Which I meant. Being

here summoned a wave of memories, most of them around how much TOM tore me down when I was growing up.

He jerked a thumb toward his shoulders. "How do you like the wings?"

Apparently we *were* going to talk about me being a dragon. "They're great. Do you want to see?" Could I invoke a little fear if I summoned my dragon?

"Now," Vidar said.

Being shot in real life doesn't work the same as in the movies. There's no barrel sliding back. No hammer being cocked. Or rather, with this army if that needed to happen, it was done before they pointed their weapons at me.

The only warning I had was the deafening *boom* that filled the room and the sharp tearing pain that rocketed through the right side of my torso, radiating from my shoulder.

I stared in disbelief at the already vanishing bullet hole in my bicep. Why did they shoot me there and not in the head? I looked at Vidar. "That wasn't nice."

Dahlia the obvious, here.

Vidar looked more surprised than me, which he manifested in a single raised eyebrow. "Nothing?"

"I hate being shot. That's something." I also wasn't as terrified as a minute ago, especially when his reaction sank in. "Oh, shit. Was that one of *the* bullets?" The immortal-slaying ones? The ammo that should have left a gaping, corrupted hole where it struck, and hurt like hell as it forced my body into a state of magical necrosis over the span of several hours?

Because I felt fine other than being annoyed my shirt was ripped.

"Nothing?" Vidar asked.

I shook my head.

"Hmm." His surprise had vanished behind a neutral mask again.

Our surroundings vanished, replaced with a vast empty field. Or rather, we'd moved, and given he and I were the only ones here and I didn't recognize the place, he'd moved us.

I barely had time to register I should be scared, when a large ball of energy knocked me off my feet and flung me back several feet.

Fuck this. I let my dragon free, growing in a heartbeat to the size of a small house. I couldn't breathe fire but I could summon it and I flung a fireball at Vidar.

He was already gone.

Another attack struck me from behind. The pain faded as quickly as it hit, leaving nothing more than the ghost of an ache behind. I couldn't maneuver in this form, and before I could adapt, magic struck me again and again. Each time in a new, vulnerable spot, tearing away my flesh before it could heal, until my dragon fled.

I fell to my knees in the dirt, choking on a haze of pain, despite being whole again. "I'm starting to feel like you want me dead." I tried to sound light, as if none of this mattered, but my words came out on a strangled rasp.

I hadn't hurt this much since the early days of school, when I suffered endless bullying at the hands of the kids who knew I hated to fight back.

"I trained with your predecessor for decades," Vidar appeared in front of me again. "Longer than you've been alive. You have no idea how to deal with me."

My fear was back, potent enough to choke on. He was right—I'd never been a great fighter. I'd absorbed my training, but I was a Noble because I was a top-notch hacker. Sure, I could kick the average person's ass, but how was I supposed to deal with a god who could assault me with an endless barrage of energy from every angle before I could adapt?

I refused to let him see me tremble. "I did okay growing up." My voice came out firm, despite everything.

"Really?" Vidar smirked. "Every one of you and your siblings, we watched you as children. Skuld and I. We knew where you were. I hesitated to bring you into the fold with the others, but Skuld insisted, and I've always wondered if it was a mistake. Skuld wondered if one of you would step up when they were gone, but to find out it's you."

Did he just imply...

No.

But he did.

I had grown up with my siblings. "Who else?" I asked.

Vidar shook his head. "It doesn't matter. Your refusal to embrace your only true gift will make you easy to eliminate, and someone more qualified will take your place. You were the Star Wars fan, weren't you?" Lightning crackled along his skin, lighting him up even in daylight.

This was about to hurt. Could he injure me faster than I could heal? I needed to get my dragon back. I needed to get out of here. I needed to do something other than succumb to my swelling panic.

A familiar growl reached my ears and some of my terror ebbed.

Fen rushed past me, his wolf lunging at Vidar, who didn't blink out of sight this time. Electricity sparked between them, lighting up the blue highlights in Fen's black fur, and casting the fighting pair in an eerie strobe.

Vidar roared and spread out his arms, sending Fen flying back.

And Frey was there, binding Vidar with magic I couldn't see, but yanked his hands behind his back.

Vidar snapped free as Fen bounded into the chaos again, his jaw snapping for Vidar's throat.

Frey jumped back, landing by my side. "Let's go."

I grasped his hand without question.

"*Fen. Now,*" Frey shouted.

Fen let out a loud howl, blood painted the landscape, and he jumped to our location.

As the clearing vanished, I swore I felt Vidar's breath on the back of my neck, and his voice whispered in my head even as NEON appeared around us.

"I am your father." The horrible, cliched words echoed in my thoughts, but were drowned out by the power I'd just witnessed. Gods fighting without breaking a sweat, wielding power I couldn't even fathom.

"Hey. You're safe." Frey crouched in front of me, and I realized I was still on my knees.

But I wasn't. Being a dragon should've made me that way. I was one of the most powerful creatures in the world.

And I still couldn't defend myself.

CHAPTER 5
FREYR

The instant I felt Dahlia again, I teleported with Fen to her location. When I saw her struggling against Vidar, all thought vanished and instinct kicked in.

My ability to bind a being was something I typically reserved for sex, but I locked Vidar in place in an instant. Fen's growl, his attack, was feral. I wasn't willing to linger long enough to find out how this would impact him. The instant Dahlia was clear and we had an opening, I brought us back to NEON, leaving Vidar broken and bleeding.

Though I doubted he'd be that weak for long.

I'd seen her vanish before, the way she did today. Both dragon and fae magic would take a section of the world and phase it to a different plane, making people invisible to magic like mine, and Vidar had discovered a way to fuse dragon magic with fae, giving him access to specific aspects of both.

Fen growled and paced as blood dripped from him, staining the carpet of our apartment. It was drying quickly, leaving deep red stains on him and the floor. "Take me back."

"No." I kept my voice firm but calm, and looked at Dahlia.

She was staring blankly ahead, not talking. Not speaking. Her wounds had healed, but it was clear more than her clothing had suffered.

"Dahlia," I said softly.

She jumped, and looked at me, eyes wide. "Thank you for saving me." Her tone was cool.

"What happened?" The charge in the air made my skin crawl.

Dahlia shook her head. "I got my ass kicked." She turned away. "I need a shower."

We couldn't keep doing this, with the not talking and her withholding important information. I grabbed her arm.

"Don't." She jerked away from my touch, eyes flashing with anger and fear. "You want to know what happened? Fine. I fucked up. I landed myself some-place dangerous, and Vidar knew how to hurt me. Even with magical dragon healing powers, he beat the shit out of me. And then..." She worked her jaw, then sighed. "I'm going to shower." She walked away.

What else was she going to say?

"I need to get out of here." Fen's tension was as visible as the tracks he'd left on the rug. "Drop me off?"

"Where?" I knew the answer, but I wanted to be wrong. There was an underground club with an entrance that changed location on a regular basis, that was straight up brawling immortals. He wanted a cage fight.

Fen raised his brows. "If I can't play and I can't use Vidar as a chew toy, I need an outlet. I'm guessing fucking is out of the question too."

It shouldn't be. I was a god of sex—I should be all for it. But he wasn't talking about the kind of passionate eroticism that fueled me. Fen wanted a battle in bed.

Sometimes the two blended beautifully. Today, they wouldn't. I wanted to ask him not to go, because I hated the thought of the violence. It wasn't fair of me to ask him to ignore that part of himself completely, but with everything going on—

"We need to talk." Aya—my sister, Freya— appeared in the middle of our living room.

Some days I swore there was a higher power, more potent than gods or the fates or anyone, pulling the strings of my life. If this *talk* was like every other one we'd had over the last year, now was one of the worst possible times to have it. "Can it wait?"

"No." Aya's gaze landed on Fen and she raised her brows. "Perhaps. Is everything all right?"

"No." Fen's growl was menacing. "But we'd love to talk."

Because there was a war coming, a battle that had been brewing for decades, that Aya seemed to know more about than most. I wanted to keep Fen away from any all-out confrontation between large numbers of immortals, but it was too late for that. We'd promised her we'd fight, in exchange for a favor.

I'd love to argue that she hadn't actually helped, last time Dahlia went missing. But Aya had been available to do so, and it was dangerous to look for loopholes when trading favors. Still, any day but today felt like a better day for this conversation. "What do you need from me, from us, exactly?"

"To fight. This isn't a war that can be sat out."

It also wasn't currently a traditional war with opposing forces facing off on a battlefield. There were fights, gods vs gods, but they were one-offs. "We have. We fought Skuld, to free you. We were prepared to fight to get Dahlia back. What fight? What is it specifically that you're pushing for?" I asked.

"I just need to know that I can call on you to fight. That you'll be there without hesitation, no matter the circumstances," Aya said. It was what she wasn't saying that I was curious about.

I stared at her in disbelief. "Not with terms like that."

"I know war is not your forte." Aya was sympathetic. "But the battle is just starting, and we need everyone."

I understood, and I wasn't going to ignore what I knew was right. "I've fought every time it's come to my door. I haven't abandoned anyone in need. But..." I tried not to glance at Fen, and failed.

"He doesn't want me involved," Fen said.

Aya stared at him in disbelief. "But you're"—she turned back to me—"he's"—

A fighter. A god of war. A being who existed to do battle. I was well aware. "I know what he is."

"Do you?" Aya asked.

She and I had clashed about the dynamics of our strengths for our entire existence. We were two sides of the same coin. The opposite ends of passion. An intense, soul-consuming love couldn't exist without a hatred that burned just as hotly.

But I'd never forget Fen almost losing himself to the beast. Becoming so engrossed in death that he nearly became the wolf rather than co-existing with it.

I was terrified of watching Fen get lost inside his own head.

"He does know," Fen said. "But Aya is right. I can't hide from this. From who I am."

And I couldn't keep asking him too. "Why now?" I asked again. "What's happening *now* that makes this so important?"

"You've seen for yourself." Her answer came more easily now that she'd had time to think about it.

I shook my head, still recognizing the deception in the one person I knew as well as myself. "No. There's something specific you're not telling us."

"Frey's right." Fen sighed. "If you're lying, I won't help."

Aya opened her mouth. "I can't—"

"Tell us the truth?" Fen asked.

She shook her head. "You need to stop coming up with excuses."

The more Fen tasted blood, the harder he would push—for the truth, for a fight...

I couldn't—

"Will you take me to see Artura?" Dahlia was back, her hair hanging in damp locks down her back. She was dressed in a baggy sweatshirt and jeans. Both unusual for her, especially in the summer.

"Now?" I could be grateful for the reprieve in conversation with Aya, but timing.

Dahlia shrugged her messenger bag onto her shoulder. "I promised you I'd talk to her about more training." Her tone was still flat and emotionless.

"Drop me off as well," Fen said.

I looked at Aya. "This conversation appears to be over." Though this wasn't the way I wanted it to end.

"It's not." Aya vanished from the room.

I knew it wasn't, and I didn't know how to reconcile the raging conflict inside, or how to help Dahlia or meet Fen halfway.

CHAPTER 6

FENRIR

Frey made me wash the blood away from the fight with Vidar before he brought me to a back alley in Manchester. The fights always took place in the fae realm, but the entrance moved from city to city. The scents of grease, exhaust, and urine clogged my nose and tinged the lingering taste of Vidar's blood on my tongue. The combination cranked the volume on the voice in my head howling *fight. Kill.*

"I'll call you when I'm done." I maintained a semblance of not-completely-bloodthirsty, for Frey's sake.

The look he gave me told me he didn't buy it. His unspoken *please stay yourself* hung heavily in the air between us.

Frey nodded, and vanished.

Conflict raged in my thoughts, making my wolf

pace more frenetically. I wasn't just hungry for a fight, I still heard Vidar's words echoing in my head. The last thing he said to her before we vanished.

I am your father.

Wolf hearing was handy sometimes. I didn't like keeping this from Fen, and I wouldn't for long. But I didn't have the mental capacity for a conversation of that magnitude.

Shouts and jeers reached my ears, the sound muffled. No human would hear the noise—the immortal-made door led to another realm and was buffered against mortal detection—but to me it was seasoning on top of the ambient aroma.

I headed toward a basic-looking metal door, one of half a dozen spanning the length of the alley, and hammered with the side of my fist. Though the door didn't have a handle, it swung open. The magic behind it would recognize my own power. When I stepped inside, it slammed shut behind me, trapping me in a metal box.

An uncomfortable tingle washed over me, neutralizing aspects of my magic.

This was a place berserkers, shifters, and anyone who needed that taste of blood could go in a world that didn't embrace violence in the same way we had in the past. There were certain rules in place, to keep us from actually killing each other—no shifting, no summoning magic, and other things.

No one remembered that in the heat of the fight,

so the rules were magically enforced. That meant we didn't have to hold back—I could grasp all the skills that were available to me.

Another door opened, and the shouts and jeers hit me full-force. *Creation* this place tasted delicious. I followed the dimly lit hallway toward a staircase that was lit at the bottom. By the time I reached the underground enclosure, I was bathed in the sensations of battle.

These fights were brief and scheduled, but they were still battles.

The woman waiting for me at the base of the stairs was petite and unassuming. Trying to focus on her was useless as she faded into the background unless she wanted to be seen. It was easier to study her out of the corner of my eye.

"Fighting or watching?" she asked.

Or, I was pretty sure she did. The words evaporated from my mind if I didn't grasp them and hold on tight. "Fighting."

I assumed she'd told me to go ahead, and I made my way toward the cage in the center of the room. Just being here fed some of my need. Being surrounded by the chaos and the bloodlust. Being immersed in it.

It wasn't enough, but the sensations were already smoothing over the fractures of discontent in my psyche.

The arena was packed to the rafters with immortals of all shapes, sizes, and powers. Fae, gods, sirens, different flavors of shifters, and a lot of berserkers. For the last century, the berserkers seemed to all but vanish. They weren't gone, not the way Valkyries were, but they were in hiding.

Odin had created berserkers for war, and that didn't exist the way it used to. But over the last decade or so, the warriors who took the shapes of bears and wolves for battle had come out of the woodwork.

Their re-emergence lent itself to Aya's insistence it was time to be ready for war, which I liked more the longer I thought about it, but it didn't answer the question of what she was hiding.

Aya was keeping secrets. Dahlia was keeping secrets. At least Frey was honest with me. I could always trust that. Of course, the thing he was being honest about was how much he didn't want me doing this...

"Beasts, monsters, and immortals, our next match is about to begin." A voice boomed through the room, magically enhanced to be heard over the crowd. Once upon a time, his intros had been long and fancy, but no one here wanted anything but the fight. Now the announcer just cut straight to the chase. "You all know Arnlaug, and a name we haven't heard in a long time, Fenrir."

The room erupted in more cheers and jeers.

I was surprised to hear Arnlaug's name. He'd

been a loyal soldier to Odin, and had been scarce since the god was killed. When my name was announced, the noise level increased several decibels. It was nice to know I had fans.

Arnlaug and I stepped into the cage and squared off against each other.

The noise of the room faded into the background, and my focus narrowed to the bear-like man across from me. We circled each other as I studied him for the slightest twitch. His every breath, the sweat trickling down his chest, and the hammer of his pulse all assaulted my senses.

It wasn't war, but it was close.

He twitched his foot, and I tensed to react. When he caught me with a feint, punching me in the chest and knocking me back, my suppressed wolf howled with rage.

I easily shook off the hit, and tightened my focus.

A foot swept under mine, knocking me off-balance, and my anger at myself for being careless surged. No more watching and waiting. I sprung forward, launching myself at Arnlaug and hitting him with a powerful punch. Before he could recover, I laid in with another hit and another.

I'd cut him somewhere. The scent of blood was in the air. It spurred me on, and I lost myself in the haze of the fight. The harder we fought, the deeper inside I reached, until I felt something invisible snap, and power surged through me.

I hit the mat face first, flattening like a plank sat on my back, despite Arnlaug not having landed a hit. The air was pressed from my lungs and I pushed to stand. Magic had me locked in place.

As the room swam back in, boos and shouts assaulted me. Some were cursing the judges and just as many spat my name in disgust.

I was hauled to my feet by an invisible hand. Rage and the need to finish the fight spilled through my veins, and I fought against magical restraints. No amount of struggling would free me, but that didn't stop me from trying.

The woman from the door appeared in front of me. She was nearly two and a half meters tall now, and the power that radiated from her was quite memorable.

"Did I piss off the unseelie mage?" I shouldn't mock her, but I was willing to pick a fight with anyone, even this creature who could incapacitate me without breaking a sweat."

"Go home, Fenrir." Her voice boomed in my head. "Cool off. Don't come back."

As the bonds fell away, so did the cage. A howling roar of frustration shredded from my throat when I realized I was standing outside NEON.

CHAPTER 7

DAHLIA

After Frey left me in front of Artura's bookstore, I hesitated outside on the sidewalk. Stupid, given who was looking for me, but my brain wouldn't shut up.

I didn't like keeping secrets from Fen and Frey, and I *would* tell them about Vidar. I'd tried to tell Magnus, but she wasn't answering her phone when I called her after my shower.

Oh, *gods* she'd fucked my father when we were on campus. And he knew what he was doing. I had siblings. I'd grown up with them. Who were they? Were they some of the soldiers who survived?

Vidar had *known*. If he was telling the truth, he'd tortured us all, and he'd tried to kill me just now.

My mind had been going like this since it cleared enough after the fight with him so I wasn't terrified.

Correction—I was still terrified. And confused. And fucked up.

And that was why I hadn't told Fen and Frey yet. I needed to wrap my brain around this and decide what purpose it served for Vidar to tell me this. Besides my current state of mind, that was.

I was here because I wanted Artura to confirm or deny what Vidar said. On the one hand, if she knew, wouldn't she have already told me? She hadn't seemed concerned about things like who the gods were in the past. On the other hand, what if she could confirm it?

Putting this off wouldn't help me, so I sucked up a few shreds of courage and walked into *The Dragon's Hoarde.*

To be far, it was a cool name for a bookstore, even more so because it was accurate. And the shop itself was an amazing collection of ancient and new books.

The sales counter was at the front of the store, and Artura was there, wearing a light sundress and a faint smile. "Dahlia. I was wondering if you were going to come in. To what do I owe this visit?"

Where to start? "I wanted to say hi. Visit my favorite aunt."

"I see."

I didn't blame Artura for not buying the answer, but I didn't have a better one yet. I also didn't have much longer to figure out my real answer.

"Clio," Artura called. "Will you watch the shop?"

A young woman stepped from between the stacks. She was stunning, with her long hair pulled into a messy bun and oversized glasses sliding down her nose. "Of course."

No, *young* wasn't accurate. She was old. She radiated wisdom and inspiration. Hearing her voice did something to my mind that felt like picking up scattered index cards and sorting them.

"Thank you," Artura said, and gestured for me to follow her to the back of the shop. She led me up a winding staircase to a small apartment.

If I didn't know better, I'd never imagine that a dragon lived here. The wallpaper was pink and off-white with flowers, and the decor matched, down to the crocheted doilies and throws that decorated tabletops and chairs.

The stacks of books, anywhere there was space, were the one thing that kept it from looking like a cliche TV grandma lived here.

"Have a seat." Artura gestured toward a pair of overstuffed chairs. "I'll get the coffee and cookies while you gather your thoughts."

"You can't just magic them out of thin air?" Last time I was here, she'd done exactly that.

She sighed. "Not unless they're prepared. I didn't know you were coming."

"I should've called. I'm sorry." I settled into a seat.

Not long ago, Artura had shown up at NEON to tell me who I was. Things had been rough between us at first—understatement of the century—as she didn't care what happened to anyone who wasn't a dragon, and I was opposed to letting everyone else die *because there would be more to replace them soon enough.*

She'd come around to seeing why I didn't want to destroy humanity and gods, though. Or rather, she'd decided my naïveté was cute and should be nurtured until I became as jaded as she was on my own.

But the point was, she'd sought me out and become the cranky aunt who was here to answer questions about dragons that no one else could. Unlike Urd who didn't give a shit I existed until she needed something from me.

Was I just as bad? I needed to come visit Artura just to say *hi* sometimes.

Artura returned with a tray holding two mugs, a stack of two plates, and a separate plate of cookies, and paused when she reached the coffee table, a frown on her face.

Every place was covered with books—there was no room for the tray.

I may have been raised an assassin, but at least I was taught manners. I hopped to my feet. "Where can I put those? Does it matter if the titles get mixed together or are they in a particular order?"

Artura almost smiled. "They can be stacked together. Just wherever there's space."

I cleared space to make room for her tray and set everything aside, trying to keep the books together and taking care to not damage them in the process.

Artura and I settled in, and I was pleasantly surprised to find she'd already added cream and sugar to my coffee, despite taking hers black. The cookies were really good too. She probably just knew how to greet guests after all these centuries, but I liked to pretend I got special treatment for being her niece.

"What can I do for you today?" she asked. "What brings you halfway around the world?"

There were so many ways to respond, and part of me didn't want to confide anything in her, especially things I hadn't even told those closest to me.

But I'd come here for a reason. I was also terrified of Fen and Frey figuring out I wasn't someone they wanted in their life, and at least on some level I was scared of losing Magnus again—she was my best friend. Might as well be my sister.

Artura, though... I already know she didn't have the highest opinion of me. "Urd came to visit me." That wasn't where I meant to start, and when Artura raised an eyebrow, I knew I should stop. "So I've met her now." *Now* I could pause. Wait for a response.

"I told her off. Like I did with you, back in the day, but maybe not so politely." Aaaand I was still talking. "She wasn't happy about that. *Oh boy* was she unhappy. And I almost got my ass kicked. By a god, not by Urd. Because I can't seem to get control over any of my dragon power except the form itself. And Vidar—the god who attacked me—says he's my father. That he and Skuld had several children. If it's true, he knows where some of my siblings are. And that he tried to kill me anyway and—"

I snapped my jaw shut. I rambled when I was feeling out of sorts, and while I'd never been able to stop the nervous talking, I had learned over the years to redirect it so I gathered information instead of giving it.

Not today, though. I'd just spilled the biggest things I wanted to keep to myself, while Artura sat quietly, sipping her coffee.

The silence that settled in the room rang in my ears. I wouldn't talk to fill that void. I wouldn't.

The longer the conversation stayed at a standstill, the more confessions bubbled up inside, until I was squirming like a child, to keep my mouth shut.

I had more control than this. "Well?" I asked.

"Is that it?"

I had no idea if she was being sarcastic. "It's more than plenty."

Artura set down her coffee mug. "Urd turned her back on you and ignored your existence, even with the series of visions about you. I did the same for a short while. There's no reason for you to offer us anything more in return."

"Except that I'm not a cold, heartless—"

Artura raised an eyebrow.

I could keep the rest of that thought to myself. "I'm not like the two of you."

"You are not," Artura said. "And my statement still stands. You did nothing wrong in turning her away."

Logically she had a point, but I didn't understand how she could take emotion out of the equation so easily. Then again, that was another reason I'd struggled with my TOM training. I could never turn my feels off. "Is it possible... Is there any way to know if what Vidar said is true?"

"Yes." Artura nodded. "I can see it by looking at you, that you have traces of him in you. You should be able to as well."

I didn't want to get into yet another way I was lacking in my dragon abilities. "So I'm not human." Like, at all.

"Of course you're not. You're a dragon."

"I'm not a very good one." If Vidar was my father —and apparently he was—did it change anything? He was still an asshole. And while he didn't have much direct involvement in my training or upbringing, he still ensured I was subjected to it.

Artura moved to a pile of books near a bookcase on the far side of the room. "I've been trying to read up on why it doesn't come naturally to you to harness your dragon."

"You have?"

"Don't sound so surprised. I told you that I'd help you and there's a reason my hoard is books."

Wait. Were dragon hoards a real thing? I thought that was just a name. "Maybe we have a few things in common after all." I had a lot of respect for someone who collected books because she actually used them.

"Perhaps we do." Artura grabbed one book, moved to another pile and grabbed a few more, and continued the path around the room. "I haven't called you yet because I haven't finished, but if you're here there's no reason to keep from you what I've found so far."

She returned to the coffee table, wiggled her fingers, and the tray of cookies disappeared. She spread the books out and perched next to me on the arm of my chair. That seemed so un-dragon-like, but I would've done exactly the same.

"These books all tell tales of beings struggling with who they are."

I picked up the newest looking one, which had to be at least a couple hundred years old, and delicately opened it to the first page. The illustrations were stunning and the language was an older dialect of Portuguese. Fortunately, I could read several languages, thanks to my training.

It took me a few pages to understand, despite being able to translate. It was a version of *The Ugly Duckling*, where the funny looking little bird grew into a beautiful swan.

Each of the other books I picked up were similar—fairytales. Fables. "These are all children's stories."

"A lot of these stories have their foundations in truth, and even those full of metaphors exist to teach children lessons about life."

Seriously? "Yeah, yeah. We all get the *just be yourself* speech about five billion times when we're kids." Except that wasn't quite true. At TOM the most important rule was *be just like everyone else. But do it better than anyone else.*

"Myopic, self-centered child." Artura's words caught me off-guard.

I stared at her in disbelief. "Excuse me?"

"Just because everyone does it doesn't mean there's not a good reason for it. And these stories have far more literal roots than you give them credit for," Artura said.

Whatever. "I still don't understand how it applies to me. Literally. Metaphorically. I know and accept that I'm a dragon."

"Do you?" Artura asked.

I clenched my jaw. This wasn't what I was here for. "I have control over the basest aspect of it." With a single thought, I changed my appearance to be the scaled cutie with wings and a tail, who still had enough control to appear human.

"That's not a dragon." With a sigh, Artura raised herself to full height—still shorter than my 165 centimeters. "That's a mockery of what we truly are."

I huffed in disbelief. "I'm not *mocking* you. I'm *adorable*."

The room around us vanished, replaced with a vast cave, and Artura no longer stood next to me. Instead, she was across from me. And above me. She was a pearlescent white dragon as big as a two-story house. "We are not *adorable*." Her voice was in my head, rather than spoken aloud. "We are fierce. The gods themselves worship us."

"I don't want the gods to worship me. I don't want anyone to do that. Being treated like an equal would be nice."

"Why?" With Artura's voice in my head, rather than spoken, it carried a whole new weight. "You're stronger than any of them."

I wasn't, though. Not if I couldn't... "I haven't always been." That seemed like a safer answer to give Artura. "I want to remember where I came from." I never wanted to be bitter and jaded like Artura and Urd, even thousands of years from now.

"You have my thoughts on the matter, and my research." Artura returned to her human form, and we were back in her living room. "I have other things to attend to. You're welcome to stay here as long as you'd like, reading the books."

I dropped the dragon parts of my appearance and flopped back into a chair the instant she was gone. Why did it feel like I was spinning my wheels —flapping my wings—and not getting anywhere? I flipped through the books slowly, admiring the art as much as processing the stories. Time passed, minutes becoming hours, as I read book after book.

So many tales of creatures born into a world that wasn't theirs, forced to conform, and then finding themselves.

I really did want that.

Did I already have that? I swore I'd been through this once before. At TOM. Because even if I struggled to be a dragon, I was the best fucking hacker they'd ever had. Why was I ignoring that and pursuing this path that wasn't working for me?

I could be figuring out why Vidar was so determined to kill me now, when he'd let me walk away before.

Fuck this, Artura was right. I needed to embrace who I was, and that meant calling Magnus, and hunting for answers the modern, digital espionage way. The way I excelled at.

FREYR

Trying to work with my mind chasing so many tracks wasn't easy, but I had a business to run and this seemed like a good time to remind myself of that. However, as I sat in my office at NEON, sifting through paperwork, focus wasn't my friend.

I hadn't heard from Frey or Dahlia all day, and while time passed differently in the realm where Frey was, I was concerned about Dahlia. I'd dropped her off this morning, and now the club was open.

She would tease me if she saw me doing this *the old-fashioned way*. I knew how to use the computer just fine, but the tactile sensations of a pen sliding over paper, and forcing my brain to work its way through numbers could be soothing.

Besides, when she was two or three hundred years old, it would be fun to see what *old fashioned* habits she hung onto. The thought was foreign—picturing someone in our future the way I was picturing her. Intimately. There with Fen and me. Not just sex, but an emotional bond.

When did that thought become so easy?

It was a far more pleasant thought than either of their moods when I took them to their respective locations.

Lust spilled in from the club, spilling through me. It should be tempting me. Drawing me into the desire pumping from the main floor and filling me with a soothing rush of energy.

Instead, it crackled over me with an anxious power that needed an outlet. That wanted Fen to push me harder rather than leave.

I flexed my fingers and turned back to my paper-work. Numbers danced in front of my eyes, and not in a sexy, seductive way.

Why was my sister pushing so hard for a loyalty that already existed between us? Why was Dahlia struggling with her dragon? What would I do if I lost Fen to his wolf? Again. Would there be a point where he couldn't come back?

None of those thoughts squashed my need and the onslaught made my skin crawl.

The air shifted and rage mingled with the ambient lust. Fen was back, and much sooner than I'd anticipated. If that mood filtered into the club, the night could fall apart. I headed to cut him off and make sure he didn't linger in the main room.

I didn't need to worry, as he found me halfway down the hall. "What happened?" I asked.

He pressed a hand to my throat and pushed me toward the nearest door—a lounge that only myself and personal guests used.

My desire spiked when he sank teeth into my shoulder when it met my neck and his growl rumbled through my skin. I didn't care why he was doing this, as long as I got to feel him. To taste him. I had enough presence of mind to detach the room from the club. I didn't want Fen or I to hold back, and it was crucial that whatever emotions Fen radiated right now didn't reach out into the club.

Fen pushed me hard enough to slam me into a wall. Plaster dust rained down around us and the supports shook.

I could ask him to calm down—though that didn't seem smart right now—or at least tell him *no*. But I didn't want that. I needed this to be rough. To hurt. I wanted to lose myself in every sensation that awaited me.

With his claws extended enough to be threatening, Fen ripped at my clothes. He cut through my trousers, shredded my boxer briefs, and tossed the ruined clothing aside. His fist wrapped around my cock tightly enough to hurt.

Creation that felt incredible. Apparently I needed

this outlet as much as he did. Time to provoke the beast. I made Fen's clothing vanish with a flick of my wrist.

It was difficult to tell if his growl was anger or desire—probably a mix of both. He pinned me to the wall again, kissing me hard enough to cut my lips into my teeth while he squeezed me by the throat.

I shoved back, sending him stumbling away a few steps.

Fen snarled, wrapped his fingers around my upper arm, and spun me away from him. He shoved me to my knees on the couch, and the legs of the furniture splintered and collapsed.

When the sofa fell, it jarred me. I didn't care. No one commanded me in the bedroom except for Fen, and I loved it when he owned me.

He pressed his chest against my back and fisted my cock. The way he jerked was rough. He yanked until my hips bucked with the need for more. Until climax swelled inside me. Until my balls were tight and I was ready to burst.

And he pulled his touch away before I came.

I grunted in disappointment, and then with surprise when he pressed his palm between my shoulder blades and shoved me forward. I had to catch the back of the couch to hold myself up, and clenched the wood so tightly it splintered under my grip.

Fen spread my ass cheeks and plunged his cock

inside me without warning. The agony was perfection. He fucked me hard and fast, digging his fingers into my hips. Slamming into me hard enough the couch rocked with each thrust.

I kept one hand on the sofa to steady myself and fisted my cock with the other. I stroked in time to Fen's pounding. The physical was good, but the raw primal lust that spilled from him was intoxicating.

He spilled inside me with a roaring howl that reverberated off the walls. His orgasm, the moment, the ambient desire in the air, pushed me over the edge as well. I beat my cock until I was raw, splattering the already ruined couch with cum.

This was the kind of buzz I could ride for weeks, and I hadn't felt anything so potent in a long time. This was my equivalent of a sacrifice. This was worship at its finest. And I'd been missing it because Fen was holding back. Not just his wolf and desire to battle, but his desire everywhere.

What had I done by muzzling this glorious creature?

CHAPTER 9
FENRIR

The red was finally fading from my mind. I could recline on the lounge sofa, Fen draped over me, and I could think again.

"What happened?" His voice was calm, almost drowsy.

"I broke security's suppression spell, and they ejected me." The entire thing almost seemed surreal now. Like I'd watched it play out through someone else's eyes. But I hadn't—it had been all me, and it was clear that trying to ignore that part of me was no longer a wise idea.

The mood in here was too subdued to tell Frey that right now.

He tilted his head to look me in the eye. "You *broke* the spell? No one does that."

I shrugged. "None of them are me."

"I can't argue with that." Frey relaxed against me again.

We reclined in comfortable silence long enough that the pleasant haze thinned in my head and reality slipped back. The feeling wasn't harsh, but it did make it difficult to sit and do nothing.

"Should we move back to the club?" I didn't assume Frey had let us break this room to pieces and fuck like animals while we were anywhere near people.

The way he sat up indicated he wasn't in a hurry to do much of anything. "Probably."

I didn't feel the shift of the room becoming part of NEON again, but I smelled the change in the air as chaos and desire clogged my senses.

And it was okay.

There was something—someone—mingled with it all. I smiled. "Dahlia's back. In the bar."

Frey stood and pulled me to my feet. "Change and go find her?"

"We could go out there like this." I didn't care that what little we still wore was torn and barely staying on, but the people out there might. Such a repressed society.

Frey shook his head. "Or we could put on clothing that has the appropriate number of holes."

"But really, that number is debatable." I really was feeling better.

Frey chuckled.

After a quick trip to the apartment for a wardrobe change, we headed back into the club. Sure enough, Dahlia was seated at a table in a back corner, looking as delicious as the first time I'd ever met her.

She had her laptop up, and it seemed like she was engrossed, but experience said she was aware of every single thing happening around her.

We approached and I slid into the bench seat across from her while Frey took the seat next to her.

One corner of her mouth quirked up, but she kept her gaze on the screen while her fingers flew across the keyboard.

"Buy you a drink, gorgeous?" Frey may be the only individual in the world who could keep a line like that from sounding too sleazy.

Though, I was heavily biased.

"No need. I blew the bartender when I got here, and he said my drinks were free."

I wasn't the only one whose mood had improved.

Frey met my gaze, amusement playing on his face. "You didn't invite us to watch?"

"You weren't here. I had to occupy myself somehow." There was a hint of teasing in Dahlia's voice, but she maintained her *I'm busy* posture.

Frey rested a finger under her chin and forced her gaze to his. "You can't even muster an apology?"

"I mean..." Dahlia shrugged. "He came in my

mouth and didn't warn me. I'm pretty sorry about that."

My snort of laughter slipped out.

Frey rolled his eyes and let go of Dahlia. "I'll have a talk with him about that. How grossly inappropriate." Even his sarcasm was playful.

"Right? That was what I said." Dahlia turned sideways in her seat and rested one leg on the bench, pressing her leg into Frey's thigh. "Apology accepted. Next time, don't put me in that position."

"Of course not, your highness," I said. "Which position would you prefer? Suspended from the ceiling by your wrists? By some well-placed ropes?"

"Hmm..." She practically purred. "Either one of those sounds like fun. Next time. And you know I was just kidding, don't you? I didn't actually blow your bartender."

I laughed. Her explaining the joke seemed so appropriate that it was the perfect punchline. "We realize."

"How did it go with Artura?" Frey asked.

Dahlia turned her gaze back to her computer and her smile vanished. "She helped me make up my mind about some things, and confirmed others."

"Confirmed what?" Frey prodded.

There was no good time to bring up this topic, and I hated holding onto it. "Confirmed what Vidar said?"

Dahlia's eyes grew wide, and then she slumped

in her seat. "You heard that? And no. But I guess also yes."

"Thank you for clearing that up." With a sigh, Frey straightened himself on the bench. "What do you both know that I don't?"

It wasn't my secret to tell, but it wasn't one I could keep. I looked at Dahlia, hoping she'd take the initiative.

"Vidar is my father. Apparently." Her words landed between us like a stone.

"I'm sorry." Frey's reply came so quickly, so sincerely, that it was almost comical. But it was also the best response I could've imagined.

I did love him.

A sad smile crossed Dahlia's face. "Me too."

That was it? Quite unlike her. "Do you want to talk about it?" I asked.

She shook her head. "I really don't. But I've been researching. Fascinating stuff. I discovered—"

The music kicked on for the next dancer, drowning Dahlia out and making my ears ring. Why did she sit so close to a speaker?

I grasped her hand, pointed to her laptop to indicate she should grab it, and Frey and I tugged her toward his office. We'd normally default to the lounge, but that needed some new furniture first.

Frey's office was large and decorated like a lot of the rest of the club—with leather furniture, and neon decorating the walls. The hooks and bars that were accessible from the ceiling weren't as obvious.

The three of us made ourselves comfortable on a corner sectional with Dahlia in the middle. She set her laptop up, revealing at least half a dozen screens overlapping each other, including a browser with multiple tabs open.

"You don't have to read them all, but you can." She gestured at the screen. "It was a lot easier than I thought to find a series of keywords. And okay, so he didn't want the kids, and yeah that makes him an asshole, but he went out of his way to keep an eye on me. On *us*, supposedly. He watched us being raised and tortured and suffering. Who the fuck does that?"

She wanted to talk about Vidar after all.

And I understood. "Loki did." I'd distanced myself from my father centuries ago, and the relationship existed in name only, but a much younger me had been in a similar position to the one Dahlia was in now. Wondering *why*? "You're allowed to feel whatever you're feeling right now."

"I'm really not." Dahlia turned back to her computer. "But I think I know where more of my siblings are. Who they are..." She bit her bottom lip. "I think I'm figuring out what kind of code TOM took from me, and I think this is the beginning of recreating it."

We hadn't been gone that long. "It hasn't even been a day."

She shrugged. "It's not a complicated script. I can do so much more with this and just a few more resources."

Something told me there was more to the situation than that, but it wasn't a suspicion I could define enough to pursue. However, if this was even a hint of what TOM had gleaned from her, no wonder they wanted her to either help them expand on the technology, or wanted her dead to keep her from recreating it.

CHAPTER 10

DAHLIA

I hadn't told Frey and Fen everything, but I'd told them enough. The longer I worked, the louder my own thoughts roared, reminding me I could burn a lot to the ground this way. TOM. Vidar. The other members of the board.

I wasn't holding back out of some strange sense of *that's not right.* Fuck them. But I wanted to make sure when I used this information to infiltrate and destroy, that I did it with a level head, rather than rushing in half-assed like a butt-hurt little girl whose daddy didn't love her.

He'd made sure I was trained better than that.

Fen and Frey gave me blank stares as I tried to explain to them what I'd done and how it worked.

"I'm trying to keep it simple." I couldn't hide my frustration.

Frey squeezed my knee. "And I have no doubt it's brilliant."

I needed another approach. "It's like Cerebro, in X-Men. But I don't need to be bald. Or wear a metal helmet."

"I get that reference." Fen grinned. Frey shot him a look and he shrugged. "What? I got that reference."

My phone rang. Magnus would get it. I hit the *Answer* button. "Jello."

"Hey. Saw you called." Her voice filtered from the speaker.

I'd done that when the shock of the fight with Vidar was still fresh in my mind. If I let my thoughts linger too long, it would rush back, along with the pain of his attacks. Which was why I wasn't letting my mind sit idle. "Yeah. Like... hours ago."

"Sorry. I got back and Kirby wanted to go somewhere, and now we're spinning our wheels and I just had a chance to check my missed calls."

Inspiration struck—this always went better with Magnus's help, and Kirby knew more about infiltrating TOM than almost anyone. "Is she still there? Are you free? You should come help me hack the system."

There was a pause and some muffled mumbling before Magnus said, "Okay. Come get us."

I gave Frey my best baby-dragon-pleading eyes, complete with a pout and batting my eyelashes.

"I'm not a taxi service." His mouth was twisted in bemusement. "Where?"

Magnus gave him a location, and it was one he was familiar with. He vanished.

What did I need to do to get my power to a point where I could pull off that same trick? Was Artura right that I hadn't fully embraced my dragon?

No. Because I could shift. Besides, today I was focusing on my true gift—digitally destroying Daddy Vidar.

Frey returned quickly with Magnus and two others. Kirby had been a classmate of Magnus's and mine—one of TOM's top assassins. Except she was also a Valkyrie, the last until she started granting the gift to Magnus and others, who had lived twelve lives before this.

She gave Fen a long hug. She'd been friends with both him and Frey in previous lives, and since finding them again in this life, she'd rekindled that relationship.

One of the gods Kirby had loved in several of those lives, Gwydion, was also with them. He gave Fen a hug too.

Kirby glanced around the office after everyone exchanged greetings. "Is this the best place to talk?"

"The lounge isn't in any condition for company." Fen's smirk implied the reasons for that were fun rather than bad.

Or maybe he and Frey were having bad fun. I jutted out my bottom lip. "And I missed it?"

Kirby wrinkled her nose. "Speaking of the things you do to furniture... I appreciate the hospitality, but I know what these couches are used for, and I'm not sitting on them."

"Wait..." A thought tickled my mind. Frey and Fen had slept with a lot of people over the centuries, and I had a hard time believing Kirby had been celibate in every single life. It never mattered to me before, but her, plus them... "Have the three of you...? Past life or something?"

"Hard no." Kirby snorted.

Frey raised an eyebrow. "Excuse me?" His tone carried an unspoken vibe of *countless people have pledged their souls just for a taste of the pleasures my cock offers.*

"But it's true," Kirby said. "Sleeping with Fen or Frey would be like... sex with a brother."

"Magnus fucked my father." The words tumbled past my lips before I could stop them.

Magnus stared at me, eyes wide. "What?"

"Who?" Kirby asked.

Right. I hadn't told anyone but Frey or Fen yet. "I had a run-in with Vidar."

"No." Kirby sounded scandalized.

"How?" Magnus asked.

Gwydion laughed. "When a mommy dragon and a daddy god each think the other is hot—"

Kirby smacked him lightly on the arm, but she was watching me. "I need you to be explicit about this. Not the sex part, please. Not when it comes to him. Vidar is your father?"

"Apparently." I chewed on my bottom lip.

"If I may," Frey said. "Since her royal queen Valkyrie refuses to sit on the sofa, the bar will be closing soon. Let's move this conversation out there. I'm going to need a drink—or ten—to do this."

Our small group relocated to the main floor of the club, where things were winding down. The bartender was so stoic—he tended to creep me out, because he just... watched. Fen told him to see to everyone else, and stepped behind the bar to get drinks for our group.

I told them about my encounter with Vidar, and the conversation with Artura after. They didn't need to know that she'd piled me down with children's fairy tales, in an effort to make light of my dragon problem, but I told them the rest, including that she'd confirmed what Vidar said.

"So she looked at you and told you who your parents were? Why didn't she do that before? Can she do that for all of us? All of us being me." Magnus finished softly.

Gwydion took a long drag off his bottle of beer. "It's not like Artura looks at you and sees your family tree. It's more like she sees your aura and recognizes the similarities to others. Like a visual chromosome scan."

Great. He knew more about my kind than I did.

Kirby covered my hand. "Does that mean you can do that too? Can you see all of me in me, or just current me?"

"That doesn't even make sense." I was stalling. Despite the confusing question, I understood what she was asking. Could I see her past lives in her aura or only her current one? But it was easier to pretend I was confused than admit there was yet another dragon thing I couldn't do.

"Is this really the conversation we want to be having at this moment?" Frey asked.

I wanted to kiss him for the redirect.

Magnus downed her shot of tequila and nudged her glass away. "I was promised we were hacking TOM. Tell me what to do."

She was pretty awesome, too.

The bar emptied as the six of us dove into research mode. Magnus looked over my shoulder, offering feedback wherever I needed it. We'd always made a great team, and this was why—she saw the things I overlooked and I did the same for her.

Kirby and Gwydion had FU specific details that tied to TOM, and Fen and Frey offered input about the gods themselves.

My fingers flew over the keyboard. Even with the multiple voices, it was easy for me to find a zone. It was as if I was connected to the machine. Like if I focused hard enough, I could reach through with my mind, tweak a few things, and magically get the results I needed.

I was mid-keystroke when a chill raced down my spine. A low growl rumbled from Fen's chest, and I swore every hair on my body stood on end.

Kirby and Magnus were on their feet in a heartbeat, summoning magical swords and spinning toward the entrance to NEON.

Bragi walked through the front door.

CHAPTER 11
FREYR

Bragi stood in the doorway to NEON, hands raised above his head. "Stop me if you've heard this one—A bard walks into a bar."

"He should've ducked," Gwydion countered.

Bragi's chuckle was strained as he cast his gaze around the room.

It was deceptive. Yes, he was facing off against some powerful beings, but he had strengths most never saw coming.

"I come in peace?" Bragi wiggled his fingers.

Fen's deep growl grew in volume. I suspected the only reason he hadn't attacked was because Bragi had helped us find and save Dahlia not too long ago.

Where I could sense lust and desire, Bragi was a full empath. When we were younger, eons ago, it made him a brilliant poet. But it weighed on him over the centuries, and he'd learned instead to project as well as absorb.

Given the assorted pieces of emotional baggage everyone in this room carried, that could be more deadly than anything Vidar could summon.

I stepped forward. "What can we do for you?"

"*Woo.*" Bragi let out a subdued exhale. "I could've picked a worse night to visit, but not much. When will you have the berserker here, and I'll come back and make sure I'm slaughtered?"

I assumed he meant Starkad, another of Kirby's lovers.

"Why are you here?" Magnus pushed.

Bragi turned his gaze on her, and a tangible layer of peace blanketed through the room. Enough that Fen stopped growling, though I still felt the tension running through him where his arm pressed into mine.

And *this* was why Bragi was dangerous.

"If you want to talk, turn it off," I said.

He shook his head. "I don't actually have a death wish. But I'll stop at this. You have my word."

"That's not worth much." Purple-black scales covered Dahlia's body, reflecting the neon behind the bar and making her look like she was glowing with the same kind of light.

Bragi tilted his head to one side and studied her. "I'm hurt. I've let a lot of things happen over the years, participated in some, but I don't lie."

"You've deceived your colleagues on the board to be here." That was a guess on my part, but when he told us where TOM was keeping Dahlia, he'd been very specific about not wanting them to know he was involved.

Bragi pulled out a nearby chair and dropped into it. He reclined, legs stretched out in front of him. "This is a no-win exchange. I point out that it suits my interests to let them think I'm still an ally, and you counter that I'll only be your ally until it suits my interests. If I tell you we don't all have sexy wolves watching our backs, you'll remind me I could've had something similar. And if I remind you that I'm not the only one who's hiding from the gods, and that you've been doing it a lot longer, you'll let said wolf rip my throat out. Hear me out and I'll give you answers, and then you can decide if I'm lying."

"We already assume you're lying. Didn't we just have this part of the conversation?" Dahlia glanced at Magnus.

Who was as tense as everyone else, but why hadn't I noticed that before? Whispers of lust—no, this was sweeter—flowed between Magnus and Bragi. It was heavily subdued, as if something— someone—was masking it from me, but it was there.

He was here because of her. That didn't mean his motives were pure, but it helped. "We're listening," I said.

He gestured to the empty tables around him. "Join me?"

"No." Kirby's tone implied her answer was everyone's.

Gwydion pulled out a seat across from Bragi.

"We're listening." I wasn't sure how long that would last, but for now he had the room's ear.

Bragi kicked back and put one boot on the table. I raised my brows and he dropped his feet to the floor again. "I signed on with TOM at a low point in my life," he said. "Anyone who's lived as long as we have, who feels anything, hits those spots on occasion." He looked at Gwydion. Fen. Me.

Bragi had a point.

"And *low point* in your case meant watching the world burn?" Dahlia didn't sound sympathetic.

"Are you really a dragon?" Bragi asked, instead of answering.

Dahlia hesitated. Not long, but enough it was noticeable. "Yes."

"Your people predicted it. Whether or not I participate, the world will burn. Or freeze, there's some debate about that. But thanks to TOM, a lot more people will die before and during." There was a catch in Bragi's voice. A twinge of... regret?

His words were a chilling reminder of the prophecies, though Dahlia had proven those weren't always true. A detail that didn't impact whether or not Bragi was willing to help extra people die.

Bragi crossed his arms. "So yes. My low point meant I wanted to see more suffering."

"That's fucked." Kirby spoke with disdain.

"I'm a fucked-up dude. Not all of us get to press the reset button on life every time it gets sucky."

Bragi wasn't just talking about Kirby, though the words were almost certainly meant to sting her. He used to love a phoenix.

"I'm here"—Bragi's tone shifted toward serious—"because I've had a change of heart. I no longer want to watch the gods destroy the good things in this world. There you have it. My big, underhanded reason." He looked around the room. Was he expecting applause? Easy-going acceptance?

I couldn't be certain what the others were thinking, but I suspected it wasn't that much different from what raced through my mind.

"You're all reformed and good now?" Dahlia asked. "You woke up one day and decided *oopsie. My bad. I'll be good now.*"

Yes. She was thinking exactly the same thing I was.

"It wasn't *one day*. A shift like that, in either direction, doesn't happen overnight. Don't pretend I'm the only person in this room who has sins to atone for." Bragi looked at Gwydion. At Fen. "Mine are more recent, but we all start the path to redemption somewhere."

"Why the change of heart?" Magnus's question

wasn't as harsh as everyone else's. The difference was subtle, but with the animosity in the room, it was distinct.

Bragi had yet to give her much attention. "That's for me to know—a god has to have a few secrets. But I'll tell you other things."

"We're listening, but you have yet to say anything useful," Dahlia said.

If this conversation was going to take this kind of time, I wanted another drink. I moved behind the bar and started pouring.

"Do you think it's a coincidence that all three of you—Kirby, Magnus, Dahlia—were brought into TOM, and became more? That Brit is what she is? What are the odds of that?" Bragi looked at Dahlia.

"I assume you don't want the boring details." This time there was no hesitation in her reply. "Very low." She spoke with the kind of confidence she'd been missing lately. "But not everyone we grew up with is immortal. Or has the potential. Or will ever achieve it, because they're dead." She finished on a harsh note.

I handed her a vodka and Red Bull, then passed out another round of drinks to everyone, including one for Bragi.

He raised his glass and tipped his head in thanks. "You're mostly correct. Did you ever meet a TOM soldier who *didn't* have the potential to become *more*?"

"How would I—"

"Have you?" Bragi cut her off.

What was he trying to get from her? What did he need to prove?

Dahlia shook her head. "I don't know. I'm not a people person, so I never spent a lot of time talking to most of the other soldiers. Besides, Nobles killed Potentials."

"You do know." Bragi set a now-empty beer stein on the table with a *thunk*. "You already have the answer. Why won't you say it? It can't be that you're afraid. Nobles don't do fear."

"*Enough*," I bit off the word at the same time Magnus did, and Fen strode toward Bragi.

"No." Dahlia's answer stopped Fen from picking Bragi up by the neck. Her voice was clear and direct. "No, I never met a TOM soldier who didn't have the potential to be more. And no, you do *not* get to tell me what I can and can't feel."

I swore her presence filled the room, though she still looked the same. I adored her regardless, but in this moment she was glorious.

Bragi smirked. "Every god on the board, every student, every soldier, every Noble, is part of TOM for a reason."

"Why are you there? Besides wanting to watch the world burn?" Fen asked.

Bragi narrowed his eyes and focused on Fen. "Do you want to find out?"

"No." I wasn't having that. Physical meets psychological? Bad idea.

"Vidar can find them," Bragi said. "Someone with Vidar's blood, who also happened to be a dragon who came into her power and was having visions, who had an affinity for the things the modern world worships, could find them better."

"Holy shit." Magnus stared at Dahlia, her mouth agape. "You really did build Cerebro."

"I told you. Wait. You know who I am." Dahlia focused on Bragi.

He straightened in his seat and leaned forward. "I didn't know, but I'd made assumptions based on the way Vidar feels about you—not good, by the way, I'm sorry—and *now* I know. Every single one of you is a threat to TOM's goal. Dahlia is a threat specifically to Vidar."

"And you're telling us this because...?" Fen trailed off.

"I don't want the world to end. We already covered that." Though Bragi never looked in her direction, the tug toward Magnus flickered stronger for a heartbeat before being muted. "Now you have the information. What you do with it is up to you."

"Well?" Fen looked at Kirby.

She shrugged. "Well, what? We've got your back, but this is Dahlia's gift."

"But you and your Rescue Rangers have a lot of

experience with this finding potentials stuff," Fen said.

Dahlia and Magnus winced.

Kirby scowled. "My *what*? There's no way *you* made that nickname up."

"What?' Dahlia asked lightly. "It's appropriate."

Kirby rolled her eyes. "As long as I get to be Gadget."

Magnus clucked. "I mean... Brit's got a rounder ass. Do you really think you could pull off Gadget?"

"How did the three of you get anything done in school?" Gwydion asked.

Like that, Kirby's irritation vanished behind a smirk. "We didn't. That's why we're not there anymore."

"You're just worried we think you're Monterey Jack," Dahlia said.

Magnus shook her head. "We don't. You're totally Dale."

"Pft." Gwydion looked unfazed. "Carry on, then."

If I hadn't lived dozens of lifetimes, and acquired a firm acceptance of not understanding most pop culture references, I'd be as frustrated as I was lost right now. Still, I was pretty sure this group had just become squirrels, not chipmunks. "Why is Vidar afraid of Dahlia?" The moment the question passed my lips, I wondered if someone would try to turn it into a riddle.

"Loki was the recruiter. Hel was the... instructor—"

"A.K.A. The brainwasher," Kirby cut Bragi off.

He gave her the briefest glance before continuing. "Vidar no longer has the support structure to recruit the people he finds. If Dahlia were to get to them first, if someone were to tell them *be yourself, have fun with life because you may just become immortal...* Vidar would be unable to maintain an army."

"Oh, *God.*" Kirby made a gagging gesture. "It's like a bad after school special. *Just be yourself to defeat evil.*"

Bragi pursed his lips and pushed to his feet. "Thank you for reminding me I didn't miss the sarcasm. Now that you have a good idea of why Dahlia's a target, I offer one of my philosophies as a parting gift—get him before he gets you. As you wacky ladies say—I'm out."

Great. He'd brought us answers—motive, goals—but that didn't get us any closer to how to deal with the situation.

CHAPTER 12

FENRIR

So much talking for so little information. It hadn't made me bitey, but I did need a nap. Unfortunately, I needed one more piece of information, too. "How are we supposed to find Vidar?"

Bragi paused and looked at me. "You have a woman on your side who can sense where people are."

"Not with a lot of accuracy," Dahlia said. "Something tells me he won't be easy to find."

"You're not trying hard enough. I've played this conversation out. Everything I've told you so far, you can verify on your own. If I tell you where Vidar is, why would you trust me? If you did decide to trust me, and you went after him and he wasn't there, you'd trust me less. Or if things went sideways, I'd hate that."

He was right about one thing—I didn't believe him. "Would you really?"

"I would." Bragi's smile was tight. "Good night." He strolled out the door.

Kirby kicked out the chair next to Gwydion and dropped into it like a rag doll. "Have I mentioned how much I hate the fucking gods?" she blew out a raspberry.

"Not in the last twelve hours. Might be a new record for you." Gwydion's voice was light as he squeezed her knee.

"He's not as bad as most of them." Magnus sounded subdued.

The fun atmosphere that was here before Bragi walked in had vanished, disintegrated in the grind of new information. "What do we want to do now?" I asked.

"Nothing's really changed, has it?" Dahlia opened her laptop again. "We were looking for Vidar before, we're looking for him now. He's still the target."

I sat next to her, searching for the right words to help raise her spirits. What popped into my head was a good indicator of how much time I'd been spending with this group lately. "You know what you should do? When you find Vidar, you should choke him on a dick."

Her almost laugh was worth it. "Not quite the way the phrase works."

"No, I think he's onto something." Magnus sat on Dahlia's other side. "But I say we take it one step further and make Vidar choke on his own dick."

At the sound of wooden chair legs scraping on the floor, I half-turned in my seat to see Kirby straightening up. "Nuh-uh. He deserves to choke on a *bag* of dicks."

"A bag of his own dicks," Gwydion said. "We'll magically clone them. He can gag on the entire sack."

Magnus snorted. "You said *sac*."

"What about a bag of dicks wrapped in used condoms?" Frey said.

The look Gwydion gave him was withering.

Frey stared back with a deep frown. "After all that, you're going to tell me *I* went too far?"

"We still have to find Vidar." Dahlia slouched on her bar stool. "He's likely not even in this realm. He's got that fucking dragon-slash-fae magic. Enough of it to hide an entire campus."

I didn't like seeing her defeated. "A campus you found."

"By *mistake*." She clenched her fists.

"But that still means that you're capable. You went to Artura to find out how to control it. How did that go?" I asked.

Dahlia clenched her jaw and stared me down. "It didn't. She told me I'm a useless dragon because I refuse to accept that I am indeed a dragon. And she's right." As Dahlia spoke, her voice grew louder. "Why would I want to be one of them? Worse, why would I want anything to do with any power I got from Vidar? Of course I'm in fucking denial about dragons being nothing like I imagined. About being related to one of the worst things to ever happen to me. Why would I want to embrace that?" She finished with a shout, her chest heaving and her nostrils flared.

"Let's take a break." Frey's voice cut through the heavy tension in the room. "Dahlia can let her scripts run, we can all get some rest, and we can talk in a few hours."

Everyone else mumbled their agreement, and Frey showed Magnus, Kirby, and Gwydion upstairs to rooms they could stay in.

When they were gone, I covered Dahlia's hand with mine, stroking the side of her fist until she relaxed it. "I've known so many people across the centuries," I said quietly. "And I've never met anyone who was as in tune with current tech as you are."

"So?" She let out a weak laugh.

"So what you were showing us before? That's brilliant technology, and you reconstructed it from the ground up in just a few hours. Set it up to run those automated searches you're so good at, and walk away for a few hours."

"But..." Dahlia sighed. "What about...?"

"It doesn't matter. Whatever you're about to ask,

it will wait. The only thing you have to do right now is set up those... ants."

"Spiders. They're called spiders." Her tone had lightened a shade.

I squeezed her hand and placed it on the keyboard. "Set up your spiders. Because no one is better at that."

Dahlia nodded, and tentatively tapped a few keys. Within seconds, her fingers were flying across the keyboard, the soft glow of her screen illuminating her pale skin.

I couldn't help but watch her work. She was such a fascinating creature—still fragile despite the immortality, but infinitely strong as well. Brilliant. Compassionate. Fierce. The way my heart swelled when I looked at her was startling and incredible.

She looked up, and I didn't try to hide that I'd been staring. Pink spread across her cheeks, looking purple like her currently hidden scales, in the glows of neon and computer screen.

"What?" She almost smiled.

"Enjoying the fantastic view."

Her blush deepened, and she closed her computer. "I'm done. Now we let it run and it alerts us if it finds anything."

"Perfect." I took the laptop, shoved it in its case, and shouldered the bag. "Let's go."

She shook her head and stayed in her seat. "I'm

going to stay down here for a bit." Like that, the hints of brightness vanished.

"Then I will too." I settled next to her again. "You can talk to me. I might understand."

Dahlia stared at the bar in front of her, tracing along the *N* etched into a coaster. "You might, at least a little. You more than anyone I know."

"Tell me."

"Why do I have to accept it? Any of it? So much of my life, that's been me—I accepted that I didn't have a choice when TOM took me in. I accepted that learning to fight was the key to survival. I accepted that being me was dangerous unless I learned how to wield my flaws as weapons. And then I realized I didn't have to. That I could walk away and be me. And do what I wanted to do and become what I wanted to become."

Dahlia scrubbed her face, leaving smudges of eyeliner in dark circles around her eyes and making her look haunted. "And now I don't have a choice. I have to be a dragon. I have to be Vidar's daughter."

"You do need to learn to control the dragon, and any power you have. It will serve you, but even if it's only so you never have to use it, you need to learn control." I would rather wrap her up and keep her safe from everything, including this, but that wasn't an option.

Dahlia clenched her jaw. "I don't know how. And no one can tell me how. At the risk of sounding like a petulant child, because *goddess* I suspect you're all tired of hearing me whine about this... It's not fair. Yeah, I know, life's not fair. But still."

"There are three types of information," I said. "The things that I would like to believe—that when this entire mess is over with the prophecies, with gods killing gods, and with what may or may not ever become Ragnarök, those of us who fought for what we believed in will be glad we did. Then there are the things I think I know—that Frey and I are one soul, forever intertwined." *That you belong there too. With us.* I wasn't sure I was ready to say that yet, and I doubted she was in a place where she wanted to hear it.. "That I would do anything to help you. Anything." That was safer.

"And there are the things I am forced to accept." I wrapped up the list. "That Loki's my father. That Hel was my sister."

Dahlia turned in her seat and her knees met mine. She kept her gaze cast down. "But you do your best to ignore the things on that last list. You even keep the kind of god you are locked away most of the time."

Ouch. "I confronted it all first. I know how to deal with all of those things."

"I'm just skipping a step."

She had to know it didn't work that way.

"You need to know how to control any power you have. You can't skip steps," I said.

She clenched her fists again, until they were pale, white stones sitting on top of black leggings. "Then maybe give me the other steps. You don't have any room to talk. Most of the time, you pretend you're something completely different than you really are."

Her petulant tone knocked loose the frustration that had been swelling inside me for a while now, and a dam burst in my mind.

"I don't *like* pretending." The words came out more harshly than I intended, but this was what we were doing, we might as well get it over with. "I don't *want* to cage my wolf."

I gripped her chin tightly enough to draw a gasp, and forced her gaze to mine. "I crave the freedom and the power that comes from letting go of the leash. I miss it so desperately that sometimes I think I might suffocate on the need." The confession I didn't know I needed, didn't know existed, flowed freely. "And I'm trying to help you, but I don't know how you can write off that feeling after only the tiniest taste."

"Then why do you lock it away? Why does Frey make you do that?" Defiance and curiosity, two of the things I loved most about her, shone in her eyes.

I relaxed my grip on her jaw, but didn't let her go. "Frey doesn't make me do this—he reminds me why it's important. I swore an oath to him to not return to that life, but I did it because if I'd stayed responsible to only myself, I wouldn't have kept the promise. I would've allowed myself to become lost in the animal, if he hadn't anchored me.

"I miss it so much. The taste of battle. The thrill of war. When I catch a hint in the air..." It fueled me. I was who I was.

"Then why do you do it? Why do you lock that part of you away?" she asked again.

How did this become about me? What she was asking me was locked away more tightly than the rest, but I couldn't ask her to accept herself while I continued to ignore me. Especially with as hard as those parts of me were pushing to be recognized.

I moved my hands to hers, closed my eyes, and grasped the memory. "When I killed Odin, there were other casualties. It was war, so that was a given, but a few of them..." Astrid, for instance. Tyr's heart. His Valkyrie. "A few of them were innocent but still died at other's hands because of my decisions." At least, I was mostly certain. Flickers of doubt haunted me, even now, centuries later.

"I lost control in my rage and grief," I said. "I slid into a pit of thinking it didn't matter. If I couldn't protect the right people, there was no reason to exercise control. For a while, I was willing to let the wolf rule, without input from me. To fight and kill indiscriminately. Frey pulled me back. He saved me. I owe him everything, so I gave him the one thing I had that meant more than anything—my word that I'd never let that happen to me again."

Dahlia turned her hands up so her palms rested against mine. Warmth flowed between us. It was a simple touch, but the connection grounded me. *She* grounded me.

Frey offered the same, but it was a different flavor.

"There has to be a middle ground, doesn't there?" Dahlia asked. "That point where you can be you, both parts of you? Because if you can't find that, then I don't know how I can be expected to."

I grasped her fingertips and traced my thumbs over the back of my knuckles. Leaning in, I pressed my lips to her forehead. "You're a far better person than I've ever been, Duckie. If anyone can do this, you can."

Her words resonated with me, though. She had a point—I needed to embrace both halves of myself. I'd hit a new type of insanity if I didn't.

CHAPTER 13
DAHLIA

I didn't let Fen lead me upstairs, but I did join him in heading up to their apartment. The conversation replayed in my mind, both the things we said and the feelings and thoughts the words evoked.

I doubted it would be easy to get over the hump of *I don't want this*, but Fen was right that I couldn't make the choice to ignore it unless I knew how to control it. Besides, there had to be a balance some-where between all and nothing. If I could grasp a command of my powers, I could pick which to set aside.

When we reached Fen and Frey's apartment, Frey was waiting inside, lounging on the couch.

Being sad, frustrated, and inept was tiring. I wanted to let some of the heaviness float away. With Frey looking confident and sexy and Fen at my back being a lot the same, I knew the perfect way to lighten my thoughts and heart. I was craving affection. Touch. Intimacy. I wanted it to be more than just sex. I needed to feel connected. To Fen. To Frey.

"Can we play?" I asked.

Frey stood and strode across the room to meet us. "Play what?" His tone was teasing. "Video games? Because I've been too old for that shit longer than you've been alive."

"No. Not video games." I had to look up to meet his gaze when he stopped right in front of me.

"Then what?" Fen asked.

I was tired of feeling lost. Like I didn't have control of my life. And I was tired of not being myself. "Something naughty." I batted my eyelashes and bit my bottom lip. "Please, Daddy?" Where did that come from? I didn't care. It was fun.

Fen's snort of laughter made it better.

Frey looked past me with a look that screamed *Don't encourage her*, and twisted my body enough to smack my ass lightly. "Never call me that again." His tone stayed lighthearted.

"Handsome?" I offered as an alternate name. "Mr. Hunky? Sir? My God?"

"Now you're getting closer." Frey kept his gaze on Fen, and his expression went blank. "What do you think?"

Fen pressed into my back, trapping me between

them in the most delicious way. "I think she asked nicely, and we should consider her petition."

"My *petition*?" I let out a light laugh.

Frey traced a finger along my bottom lip. "She did ask nicely."

"But she was also vague." Fen grasped my wrists and gripped tightly enough to sting.

Yum.

Adding a second finger to the mix, Frey pressed both into my mouth. "*Naughty* can mean a lot of things."

I couldn't talk on account of having my mouth full, so I sucked instead. Besides, listening to them debate my fate was fun.

"Sneaking cookies before dinner is naughty." Frey studied me.

I looked back, eyes wide and as innocent as was possible while licking his fingers.

Fen trailed his nose up the side of my neck, and his audible inhale sent shivers of anticipation up my spine. "Luring little duckies to your apartment with the promise of cookies is naughty."

This was exactly what I wanted. I pulled away from Frey's fingers to speak. "Do I get cookies? Don't get me wrong—I like cookies—but I meant *naughty* in more of a rough fucking kind of way." I paused. "And cookies after."

One corner of Frey's mouth twitched, but he recovered his stoic expression quickly. He looked past me again. "Stripping someone down on the balcony, just before the sun rises, is naughty."

The sun wouldn't be up here for a few more hours, but Frey had the ability to open a doorway to anywhere in the world, and he loved picking different locations to look out over various cities. And balcony sex? Always a favorite of mine.

"What location did you have in mind?" Fen asked.

I couldn't help myself. They started it, and now I was craving sweet to go with my spice. "Someplace with cookies?"

Fen's laugh was throaty and filled me with anticipation.

"New York," Frey said.

The sun wouldn't be up there for a few hours either, but in the city that never slept, at three am, fucking dozens of stories above the street sounded incredible. Frey grasped my fingers and led me to the door, Fen staying behind me. We stepped outside, to lights far below. The height was dizzying and incredible.

Frey stripped away my clothing a piece at a time, slowly, teasingly, while Fen kissed along each bit of freshly exposed skin. Hands and mouths roamed my body while New York moved on below us.

When I was naked, Frey pressed his body to mine. The texture of his clothing was tantalizing against my bare skin. He cupped my cheeks, teased his thumbs over my cheekbones, then glided his hands down my arms, pushing them behind me as he moved.

Cold metal hit my wrists, followed by the clank of chain on steel. Frey had handcuffed me to the railing. "You wanted naughty," he said. "Naughty girls get cuffed."

I tugged at the restraints, but not too hard. My fake pout turned to shock when Frey and Fen stepped away from me. The chilly air rushed around me, kissing my skin and leaving me wet and wanting. It was delicious.

Especially when the men moved their attention to each other. Seeing them kiss, peel away their clothes, and stroke each other's cocks made need throb between my legs.

I couldn't do anything to ease the need but squeeze my thighs together. My nipples ached for attention. My body shivered with want as much as from the cold. Watching the light power struggle as Frey pushed into Fen and Fen pushed back, drew a whimper from me.

Frey looked up from a drawn-out kiss, and met my gaze with a wicked smirk. "We didn't forget about you," he said. "Tell me what you want."

"Lots of fucking and orgasms." I was tired of being coy.

"Beg me for it."

That one word almost killed my mood, and I

wasn't sure why. Most of the time, I'd play and I'd beg, but tonight... "No."

Frey raised his eyebrows.

"I'll ask. I'll tell. But I will *not* beg. Not this time."

Reaching behind me, Fen snapped the link between the cuffs rather than unlocking them. He wrapped an arm around my waist and pulled me into him, so my back met his chest. "The lady has spoken."

The heat of his frame warmed me, and the well-muscled hardness teased me.

"So you have." Frey's smile was heat wrapped around me and also sent a shiver racing through me. He placed a finger under my chin to tilt it up and brush his lips over mine. I felt the kiss in my toes, and I knew what it meant to be claimed.

Fen slid his hands up my sides and light kisses along my neck turned to nibbles and then rougher biting.

Never taking his mouth from mine, Frey slid a hand between my legs. When he parted my folds, I groaned in anticipation, and when he teased my clit, my entire body bucked into his touch. He wrapped his fingers around the swollen bud and stroked. Fen cupped my breasts and rolled my nipples between his fingers as he sunk his teeth into my flesh.

The focused attention from both of them pushed me into pleasure, coaxed me toward the edge of orgasm, then sent me tumbling over with a scream of delight. Frey didn't let up, circling my clit until my body hummed and quivered and felt like it might melt.

Frey glided a hand along my thigh to my ass, then slid lower. He pulled my leg to hook on his hip. When he slid his cock into me, his groan lit my senses on fire. He rested inside me, unmoving aside from the occasional twitch. Another delicious agony of anticipation.

Fen glided slippery fingers along my ass, generously applying lube to my rear entrance. I wasn't going to ask where he got it—presumably from the same place as the handcuffs. The two of them probably had toys and other implements stashed on a lot of their balconies.

When Fen was done, he nudged my hole with the head of his cock. I forced myself to relax and let him enter me slowly.

It felt incredible to be held between them, both of them inside me and the three of us joined. They rocked to a slow in and out in an easy rhythm, and then thrusting became a heated friction. I draped my arm around Frey's neck for balance.

He pressed his lips to the hollow of my neck, behind my ear. "Play with yourself," he said. "Make yourself come while we're buried inside you."

I wasn't sure I could climax again, but I was willing to try. I fingered myself, but my clit was both too tender and simultaneously numb from the previous attention.

Frey pressed a hand to my throat and squeezed enough to fuzz my thoughts. My head grew light and my body was one giant nerve. I was floating above the world. It was easy to slip into all the sensations as another orgasm filled me.

I felt when Frey finished. Heard Fen. I didn't pull my hand away from myself until they'd stopped thrusting and grunting. This felt incredible.

Fen nuzzled the back of my neck, drawing my attention but not yanking me from the warm fuzzy feeling. "Duckie?" His voice was soft.

"Mhm?" I was so happy right now. So safe.

"Neither Frey nor I can fly."

That was an odd thing for Fen to say. Why didn't I feel the ground under my feet? I looked down to see the city—the balcony—far below us. Holy. Shit. "How are we..." *floating*?

"It's all you." Frey sounded awfully calm for a naked man who's supposed only means of being up here was the incompetent dragon he'd just fucked.

But I wasn't terrified. The longer the thought sat in my head *we're flying* the more my heart hammered out a happy beat against my ribs. "We're flying." The words tasted even better out loud than in my head.

"*You're* flying," Fen murmured against my skin.

I wasn't clinging to them. They weren't falling. It seemed that just touching me... And we were... "*I'm flying!*" My shout vanished into the night. Fucking flying. Flying while fucking. Air rushing around us. The chill biting into our naked skin. "Holy shit."

"We should probably land before we talk more about this." Frey had a good point.

I didn't know how to land. Nothing in comic books or movies or comic book movies had prepared me for taking the entire group down slowly, while we were naked and intertwined, without crashing.

Fen squeezed my shoulders. "You've got this."

I didn't doubt for a second that he believed that. Closing my eyes, I focused on *lower us slowly until we're on the ground.* I didn't dare look, but it didn't feel like we were moving. There should be wind rushing around us as we plummeted to the ground, shouldn't there?

Solid ground brushed the soles of my feet, and I dared peek. We were back on the balcony.

Excitement pulsed through my veins and my heart hammered against my ribs. If this was what a taste of flying felt like, of my real power, I had no idea how Fen and Magnus ever locked it away.

CHAPTER 14

FREYR

Dahlia's moods tended to be infectious, especially her enthusiasm. When combined with the buzz of incredible sex, her joy at having flown was an intoxicating high.

"I want to go again." She stood at the edge of the balcony, her hands on the top of the iron railing that kept us from plummeting to the streets below, and her feet on the bottom rail. She should be pale against the backdrop of a pre-dawn sky, but scales shimmered over her body, almost camouflaging her.

I wrapped a hand around her waist and pulled her back. "Not in the middle of the city."

"Aww." The way her bottom lip jutted out was adorable. "Can we go someplace I can just try? Please? I need to know if I can do it again. I need to know if it was a fluke."

If it was real, she should be able to take us wherever she wanted to go, but I could think of half a dozen reasons suggesting that was a bad idea.

"Let's go. Our guests are resting, and it will only be an hour or two." Fen looked at me with wide, pleading eyes.

It didn't matter how old the wolf was, when he gave me the fucking puppy dog eyes, I couldn't refuse. The atmosphere around us was light and warm and I wanted to preserve that. I gathered their clothes, grabbed their hands, and took the three of us to an isolated beach in northern Europe.

This was another of Fen's favorite places to let loose, with the ocean in front of us and a dense tree-line behind us. But this place didn't have recent bad memories associated with it.

The instant we appeared, Fen and Dahlia shifted. She was a full dragon, not a woman with a tail and wings, but she also wasn't huge. She'd kept her size about the same size as Fen's, and she hovered in the air a few meters above him.

And then she was soaring high above the trees, and Fen was chasing her. He bounded up trunks and snapped his jaws at her clawed feet, always playful. When she swooped out over the ocean, he ran as far into the water as he could without stumbling, then circled until she glided back toward him.

It was both comical and majestic. The combination of playful youth and ancient, stunning beauty was so perfectly Dahlia that it was incredible to watch.

Had it only been a day or two since we did this with Magnus? Since Dahlia was climbing trees in an attempt to taste what she was living in its full glory now? The last forty-eight or so hours were a blur in my mind. A compressed spot of chaos.

Out here, the scents of salt and water and pine, mingled with Fen and Dahlia's laughing growls, helped chase the haze away.

I blinked home long enough to fetch us a blanket, and laid it out in a warm spot of sand. When Fen and Dahlia came back, they were human again. The only thing any of us wore were tired, goofy smiles. It was so easy to spoon myself around Fen while he held Dahlia. So calming.

She was so much a part of who we were now, I couldn't imagine her not here. When did that happen?

I didn't realize we'd fallen asleep until an insistent chime woke us up. The sun was resting on top of the horizon now, reflecting a stunning palette of orange and purple in the water.

"What do you want?" Dahlia mumbled, her eyes closed as she groped the blanket around her, and us in the process.

I loosely grabbed her wrist. "I believe that's your phone." I pressed my lips to her bare shoulder.

"It is." She sat up and finally opened her eyes.

Fen stayed reclined in his spot, watching both of us with a sleepy, relaxed expression. "Where are you hiding it?"

"Hiding what?" she asked.

"Your phone. I would have noticed if you had it on you." He looked her over.

Dahlia patted herself down and squirmed on the blanket. "Nope. Not up my butt."

I nodded at the pile of clothing I'd brought with us. "I'm guessing it was in your pocket."

"Oh yeah." Dahlia rolled onto her hands and knees and crawled toward the chime, her bare ass wiggling in the air. She dug through the stack, extracted her phone, and scowled when she saw the screen. "Fuck."

While the exclamation wasn't happy, she also didn't sound too distressed.

"What's going on?" I asked.

"Most of these are from Magnus. Asking where we are. If we're coming back. If we went to kill Vidar without her. Threatening mutiny... Can she mutiny if we don't have a captain?" Dahlia swiped her thumb over the screen as she talked. "Oh. And my spiders found something."

"*Something* is vague." I tossed Fen his pants, and pulled on my own clothing.

Dahlia dressed as well. "I won't know *less vague* until I get back to my computer." She paused and looked around us. "This was really amazing. I can't believe… I did it."

"I knew you could." Pulling her close, I pressed my lips to her forehead.

Her grin was more stunning than the sunset. "Can I take us back?"

I opened my mouth to answer.

She kept talking. "I know I can do it. I promise. And if I do it wrong, you'll be there with me to fix it immediately. *Please.*"

"Yes." That had been my answer anyway. Did I think her mastery of the skills would be as simple as it appeared? No. But something had clicked for her, and the only way for her to keep making progress was for her… to keep going. I took her hand. "You've got this."

We vanished from the beach and reappeared in our apartment. The instant we were tangible again, panic flooded me. I couldn't sense Dahlia. Logic was still there, too. I could feel her hand. I could see her. But her presence was a blank void.

She was watching me with a neutral expression. This was a surreal feeling. I could stare right at her, but that sixth sense that I relied on so heavily insisted she wasn't in the room with us.

"Is it working?" That was her voice, coming out of her mouth.

I nodded slowly. This happened when Artura

didn't want me to find them. When Vidar hid Dahlia away. "Are you doing this?"

"Yes." Her grin was back and abruptly, so was her energy, flooding the room with bright, high-energy warmth.

"Fucking amazing."

We took quick showers and Dahlia checked her computer. She refused to share the results until we were with Magnus. "She'll never forgive me if we dive into the good stuff without her."

We found Magnus in the diner next door to the club. This place was mine, as was the whole block, but it was more open to the public than the burlesque club, in more ways than one.

She was sitting in a booth at the back, a half-eaten plate of nachos in front of her. When she saw us, her scowl deepened. "They tried to kick me out," she said when we were within hearing range. "Said they needed the seats." She looked around the dining room, which only held a few other people besides employees.

"I'll have a talk with the manager." I slid into the booth seat across from her and Fen sat next to me.

Dahlia took the seat by Magnus. "Where are Kirby and Gwydion?" Dahlia asked.

Magnus wrinkled her nose. "They said they had other things to do, because you bailed on them."

"Shit." Dahlia huffed. "I'll apologize to her. But I promise it was for a really good reason."

"Hot sex is not a good reason for standing people up," Magnus said.

It was in my line of work. "I beg to differ."

"We weren't having sex." Dahlia paused and twisted her mouth. "We didn't stand you up because of the sex." From a certain angle, she looked like she was vibrating in her seat at high frequency. "I was flying."

Magnus's jaw dropped. "No. Like, in a plane?" A hint of teasing slid into her voice.

Dahlia stuck her tongue out. "*No*. It was all me. As a dragon. I figured it out. I was fucking flying."

"Oh my God, *yay*." Magnus hugged her tightly. "Totally valid reason for going missing. How was it? It's amazing, isn't it? Did you love it?"

"*Love* isn't a strong enough word. I don't think they make a word that says how incredible it was." Dahlia was all grins.

I wanted to let them compare notes all day, but we did have other priorities. "I hate to interrupt, but what did the computer say?"

"Right." Dahlia placed her phone in the center of the table. "This is where our target is." The screen showed a map, zoomed in to the center of the Black Sea.

I hated to rain on her good mood. "Was he on a boat? How do we know he's still there?"

She switched to a different screen. "He is. And

that's probably not water where he is. He's not in this realm."

"How...?" Admittedly, my understanding of technology barely ranked above what most people's grandparents grasped, but tracking someone digitally should require they be in a place with a digital signature. Internet. A network. Something like that. Though we'd seen tech in TOM facilities that weren't in this realm, Dahlia insisted those computers weren't connected to anything in this world. "I thought you couldn't find computers in other planes."

Magnus was smirking. "This is why Dahlia's so amazing. Technology can't find them, but apparently she has the magic to do so."

"Which means my not-Cerebro works better than I thought." Dahlia clapped twice.

It was brilliant, it was magic I'd never seen before, and it explained why she was a threat to Vidar.

"Last time we walked into one of these TOM facilities that was in another realm, it was abandoned," Fen said. He was talking about when Dahlia was taken, to get more information out of her about this same tech. "How do we guarantee we won't run into that again?"

Dahlia jabbed at her screen. "That's Vidar. That's what the program looks for. He's—" She jabbed again, her giddiness tarnishing.

"This is like any other op. We do recon first." Magnus sounded sorry to have to say so.

If war wasn't my thing, sneaking into enemy bases *really* wasn't my thing. "Can we do that? Get an in-person confirmation without him knowing?"

Magnus twisted her mouth. "Maybe."

"And what's your plan if you do?" I asked.

Fen's carefree expression from the impromptu play earlier was gone, but his smile wasn't. "If the timing is right, we take him out. Otherwise, we regroup, make a battle plan, and *then* take him out."

"Are you sure?" My question was for Dahlia. If she was still processing the news about her relationship to Vidar, she may not be prepared for *take him out.*

She nodded. "He's not actually Darth Vader."

"*Ha.* Darth Vidar. I get it." Magnus's excited exclamation cut through the tension. She looked around the table. "Sorry. I just got it."

Dahlia sighed. "He doesn't have a redemption arc. It's not like we're going to blow up the facility and he's going to turn good at the last minute." She almost sounded like she regretted that. "Speaking of, we shouldn't blow anything up. He's an asshole, but that doesn't mean the soldiers deserve his fate. We should kill him, though."

"As far as getting in without being seen, Dahlia's the best answer."

I stared at Fen in disbelief. "No."

"She's an expert at recon," Magnus said. "And if she can do dragon stuff now..."

"I can." The waver in Dahlia's voice wasn't reassuring. "You saw it upstairs. I can teleport in and get out quickly and he'll never know I was there."

I hated to shatter her newly found confidence, but—

"Last time you tried 'porting, he almost killed you," Magnus said what I was trying not to think.

Dahlia scowled at her. "Are you on my side or not? I have it under control now."

"You flew. You didn't do anything else. What happens if you don't come back?" Magnus's voice grew quiet, making it difficult to hear her as she trailed off.

"I can feel it. I've got it." Dahlia was insistent. "It's like everyone keeps saying. I just know how. Besides, what's the alternative? We play to people's strengths and this is one of mine now. We need someone who can get in and get out without being seen, that's me."

Not long ago, I wouldn't have thought twice about arguing with her. She *was* highly trained. But this was different. What she meant to me was different than not long ago as well. I opened my mouth to make one request.

"If you go, you're not going without me." Fen beat me to it.

Dahlia nodded. "That I will do."

CHAPTER 15

DAHLIA

I didn't quite understand why I could do all the dragon things now. The power was there and I could feel it. There was understanding and acceptance, like a switch had been flipped.

But I didn't know where the switch was or how it had happened, and I was terrified that it wouldn't take much to flip it off again.

Fen and I had a plan for recon, but I needed a few things from the apartment I shared with Magnus before we went in. Though I spent a lot of my time with Frey and Fen now, it wasn't officially *home*.

NEON felt more like home than any other place ever had, but it wasn't official.

I took Magnus with me to the apartment. Appearing in the middle of the living room, knowing that I was the one to bring us there, was strange. So was the darkness. The silence except for the hum of the fridge. The heavy air.

"We should air this place out." Magnus's soft voice was startling in the middle of the stillness.

I nodded. "Maybe do some dusting."

"Definitely empty the fridge."

"Why do we keep the place?" I asked.

The frown she gave me cut deep. "Because it's ours."

I saw that she was upset, but didn't understand why. "It's not. It's a few rooms that we rent that we never sleep in."

"*You* never sleep here. I don't have big scary gods begging me to fuck them every other night." Magnus almost sounded...

"Are you jealous?" I felt silly the instant I asked.

Magnus sank onto the couch, which was really an old futon we'd rescued from someone's trash heap and covered with a thrift store quilt. "Yes. No. Maybe? I don't know. Don't take Fen on this mission. Take me."

"Don't. Please." I made the request before I understood what I was asking.

"Don't what?"

She and I were partners. Had been since Hel decided we had the best chemistry to work with each other. Which in that instance meant we were the worst at being Nobles. "Don't ask me to choose between you and Fen." There it was. Magnus meant different things to me than Fen did. Than Frey.

I needed all three of them in my life, and while her question was only about one mission, it was tied to more.

"We're partners," Magnus said.

"And if this was a normal mission—normal recon—it'd be you and me in a heartbeat. I swear to you. But Fen... He's a killer." And I needed that backing me up. Besides, he wasn't going to let me go without him.

Magnus scowled. "*We're* killers."

I hated the way she said that so quickly. So easily. "We walked away from TOM because we don't like killing."

"No, but we know how. I can shield you when we're in there." She has the ability as a Valkyrie to create a magical shield.

I sat next to her on the futon. "This is just recon." It was a weak argument, considering the rest of the conversation.

The twist of disbelief on Magnus's face said she noticed. "It's not *just recon* if you're taking him because he doesn't mind killing. I'm worried about you. About this mission. I have a bad feeling about the whole thing, and you and I have each other's backs. Always, but especially against Vidar. Against anyone on the TOM board."

"And when we go head-to-head with him, you'll

be there. I won't face Vidar without you," I said. "I wouldn't dare ask you to miss out on kicking his ass."

Magnus leaned her head on my shoulder. "Come back from this. Alive. Safe. Kirby and her people are fun, but..."

"They're not you. I know. Fen and Frey live in a different place in my heart than you do. You and I are sisters forever." I squeezed her hand.

"If he doesn't bring you back, I'll find a way to kill him." The shift in Magnus's tone was abrupt, from wistful to sharp and threatening.

"I know. I'd do the same for you."

Magnus and I finished gathering the clothing and gear I needed for the mission, and I took us back to NEON.

After a double and triple check that included me practicing barked orders to use different powers, Fen and I decided we were as ready as we could be with the limited time we had.

My brain was a wreck, but I managed the focus I needed to take Fen and me to the location my program found. I felt Vidar before we left. I knew we were heading to the right place, and even sensed a hallway free of people, for us to appear in.

The instant we appeared, I hid us. It was a strange sensation, keeping us in an alternate plane, but also making sure we stayed outside of it. Water existed in the regular world, in the same spot we stood now. Keeping us phased between realms, I swore I felt the sea pressing in on us, even as we sneaked through hallways, watching the TOM soldiers around us

I didn't trust the combination of my magic and everything flowing through the facility to keep us hidden, so Fen and I stuck to shadows and empty halls. There was already one flaw with this plan—my magic and my program didn't pinpoint Vidar to a single spot, both just recognized an overall aura of where he was.

So we crept through hallways, avoiding everyone and following what I could only describe as a scent, but made of energy.

After checking every room we could find in the facility, and one of the tensest hours of my life—which was a high bar—we had to admit Vidar wasn't here.

We returned to NEON, to Frey and Magnus's relief and with me feeling intense disappointment that we didn't find anything. Not only that Vidar wasn't there, but that my magic, my program, hadn't worked.

The next several days were more of the same. I'd set my spiders to search for Vidar, confirm their results myself, and Fen and I would do recon that turned up nothing.

"I don't get it." I was in the recently refurnished lounge behind the club with Frey, Fen, and Magnus as we discussed Failed Mission Number Four. "I can *feel* him there, every time." I swore at this moment I could hear all of them asking if I really had the grasp on my powers that I thought I did. It was probably a good thing I couldn't actually read minds. "My dragon stuff is working. You've all seen it. It's not like I'm bad at this still."

"No one's questioning you." Fen's voice was tight. So many sneaking around missions with no action had to be driving him insane.

I sank lower in my beanbag chair, hoping it would consume me. "I am."

"I have an idea, but no one's going to like it." Magnus picked at the loose threads around a thin spot near the knee of her jeans.

I was up for most anything at this point. "Let's hear it."

"We call Bragi."

Except that. At least she didn't suggest we call Vidar. But Magnus didn't usually make rash decisions. I trusted her with most everything, though she hadn't always picked right when it came to the gods who raised us. "Why?" I was sincere.

"It doesn't matter *why*. As you ladies would say, that's a hard no." Frey was reclined next to Fen on a new couch.

They'd tried to tug me over there with them, but I wasn't exactly feeling worthy of that kind of closeness. I shot him a look to convey he needed to not jump to conclusions. "I want to hear her out. Why Bragi?" I asked.

Magnus leaned forward and rested her elbows on her knees. "He knows how their operation works, and the information he's given us so far has panned out. Besides... I have a feeling we can trust him."

I wanted to trust Magnus's gut. She'd saved my skin more times than I could count over the years.

"He was clear about not telling us more, the last time he was here. It seems like the perfect setup, to feed us good information, just enough to make us want more, and then drop a bad lead," Fen said. And he was right.

I *wanted* to trust Magnus, but this time the signs weren't in her favor. "Bragi has also low-key stalked us—you—since we left TOM, and rarely done more than offer vaguely threatening, not quite helpful comments."

"He told you who you were." Magnus scowled.

I gritted my teeth and stared back. "I know who I am."

She sighed. "What are our other options? What we're doing isn't working. We can't sit around and wait for Vidar to come for you. You don't want to trust Bragi? I'll go to him myself. I'd rather walk into a stupid trap and take the enemy out then, than wait for him to destroy you."

"I vote for that thing she just said." Fen pointed at Magnus.

Disbelief spilled through me and I looked at him. "You vote for the *let's get trapped* plan?"

"I vote for the *let's stop sneaking around, and kill something instead* plan."

Frey shook his head. "No."

"Let's take a vote. Everyone in favor of confronting this head-on, aka, calling Bragi, raise your hand." Her hand shot into the air and so did Fen's.

Frey's frown was the kind of expressions artists preserved in stone for centuries. "I vote against that option."

"There are only four of us," I said. "If I vote with Frey, we'll have a tie."

Magnus shrugged. "If you vote with Frey, you have to offer an alternative. I think that's fair."

I didn't have an alternative, and I wanted this done. Besides, I was a fucking dragon, and I could do a lot of things I hadn't been capable of last time I faced Vidar. "Fine. Let's call Bragi."

CHAPTER 16

DAHLIA

I was surprised when Magnus called Bragi and he not only picked up, but agreed to meet with us. My shock turned to *yeah, that sounds about right*, when he showed up and told us he didn't have any more information to offer.

I set up a projector in the lounge so we could put up maps or any other information we needed, to talk through locations and next steps.

Bragi walked back and forth between the light source and the image. "Make this 3D."

"This isn't the movies. I'm not Tony Stark." I wasn't giving Bragi any leeway. It already rubbed me wrong that I saw no choice but to agree to his being here.

He looked me over with a gaze that made my skin crawl, then turned to Magnus. "Genius emo with a cute redhead who does half your thinking for you... You might be."

"Goth," I corrected him. "And she's not cute, she's fucking gorgeous."

Bragi shrugged. "She is. Try this on." He snapped his fingers and my projected map became a giant hologram in the middle of the room.

I refused to be impressed. Partly because he'd shown me up, and just as much because he needed to keep his distance from Magnus.

"Where have you been so far? Which bases?" Bragi's light show had pinpoints all over its globe, at least a few of which I knew were TOM facilities.

I was a little terrified they might all be. "There aren't enough soldiers to occupy that many spaces," I said.

"Not all TOM, and not all facilities. FU safehouses here, here, here"—as he talked, he pointed— "TOM ones here and here. FU bases. TOM allies." He clicked one spot in Australia and zoomed in tighter, right on Perth. One dot became three dozen.

Holy shit, they were everywhere.

"I only know what some of these are. I can tell you who they're affiliated with, but not what they're used for. I don't know if any one person has all of that information. But if you tell me where you've been, I can help you narrow things down," Bragi said.

Fen's *hmm* was as much growl as anything. "No.

Tell us why Dahlia thinks she's found Vidar when she hasn't."

Bragi hesitated a heartbeat before saying, "I don't know." There was no way his poker face was that bad.

"Liar." I was happy to call him on it.

Bragi stepped closer to Magnus. "When you walk through a room, that faint perfume you're wearing leaves hints of you behind. It's you mingled with someone else." He leaned his head in close enough to inhale.

Magnus bit her bottom lip. "I'm not wearing perfume."

Was this what it was like watching me with Fen and Frey? No, because there was no threat of them betraying us.

"You are," Fen said. "Just a hint, freshened up about half an hour ago. Except the scent you leave behind—that anyone leaves behind—is more of a shadow than the same smell. Even potent perfume doesn't smell the same on a person as it does once they leave a room, so if Bragi is saying a magic signature is the same..."

"What I'm sensing is strong when we look for Vidar. My magic is working fine." I didn't like the implication to the contrary. Besides, I'd already considered what Bragi was proposing, and been doing quiet tests with the people around here, to see if I could tell the difference between how they felt in a room and how a room felt once they left.

I could.

"Dahlia, close your eyes," Bragi said.

As if. "No." My answer came out on a laugh of disbelief.

"Magnus?" he asked.

She complied without question.

I didn't care for any of this. Especially when Bragi brushed his fingers along her neck, and lingered. I'd ruin him if he hurt her.

"Do you feel that?" Bragi's voice was low. Seductive.

Magnus nodded.

Bragi dropped his hand away and took a few steps to the side. "How about now?" His voice still sounded like it came from next to Magnus.

"Yes," she said.

"Vidar is doing the magical equivalent of throwing his voice." This time Bragi's voice came from Bragi's mouth.

Magnus's eyes flew open and she whirled toward him.

Pieces clicked in my mind. Vidar was playing with me. "He can tell when I'm in one of those places, even if I'm hiding."

"Likely, yes."

Fuck. Fuck. Fuck. "So every time Fen and I go somewhere, it's because he wants me there, and he's just sitting back and laughing?" I hated this. All the mind games. All the complications. All the twisty, turny, movie-level stupidity just to... what? "Is he testing me?"

"Only Vidar knows why he does what he does," Bragi said. "I assume some of it has to do with destroying you before you take him down. Some of it is probably vengeance against Fen. Presumably Vidar's a little bored as well."

Everybody at TOM had learned the story of how the Big Bad Wolf Fenrir Slayed the Mighty and Righteous Odin.

The story we'd been taught in school was nothing like the one Fen told—go figure—but he had dealt the killing blow to Odin in both tales.

"We need to force this confrontation," Fen said. "Do we pick one of these locations, go stand in the middle of the building, and shout for his attention? We're not going to sit here waiting for him to decide it's time to come after Dahlia."

"Or you," Frey added.

Fen shrugged. "At least then I'd know where to find him."

"That exactly." Magnus pointed at Fen. "Wait." She frowned and squeezed her eyes shut. "Pull up a flat globe and plot out all the places we've been so far."

I was already working before she finished talking, because I knew exactly where she was going. "Holy shit, you're right."

"Care to fill us in?" Frey asked.

Gods were as superstitious as anyone. They liked their symbols, especially those that gave them power or took it away from someone else. For instance, the original TOM campus had been laid out like a sacrifice circle, because a sacrifice was needed to free the god locked beneath.

I pointed to the dots on the map, and connected them as I did. "Do you see it?"

Bragi sang something softly that sounded distinctly like, *and Bingo was his name.*

Fen glared at him, then turned back to the computer. "The sigil on Vidar's churches."

"Arrogant fucker." The only thing that surprised me about the discovery was that I was related to the arrogant fucker. "We've basically been hitting each mark in order, based on how the sigil is drawn."

"What if we skipped ahead one?" Magnus finished my thought.

I lit up the TOM facilities Bragi had given us, and used the type of facility to narrow down our options. We were left with two choices for a destination, based on our logic. "If we do this and anyone sees us besides Vidar, we'll need a new angle," I said.

Fen squeezed my shoulder. "Does it feel right to you?"

"You're not hesitating now, after all this, are you?" Bragi's tone was taunting. "Is this why you were *doing recon* before you made each play? Did you want to ensure Vidar knew you were looking for him?

If he was trying to get under my skin, or get me to decide with some sort of reverse psychology, I was perfectly capable of thinking myself out of the situation without his help. But I felt *something*. It was time to decide. "He's there," I said. "Let's go."

"Great. See y'all 'round." Bragi's hologram disappeared.

Frey grabbed his wrist before he could do the same. "How about you stick around," Frey said. "You've been pushing a confrontation like this for a while. Now's your chance to see how it turns out."

"And your chance to kill me if it doesn't go well. I get it. But you have a point—I would like to see Magnus and Dahlia win this one." Bragi settled into a nearby chair.

I felt like an afterthought in his statement, but he hadn't even mentioned Fen or Frey. Why was he here? I still didn't understand or believe the motivations he'd given us, but asking him hadn't offered any additional insight so far.

Planning didn't take long. We'd been ready for this fight for days, and I knew how to work side-by-side with Magnus and Fen.

I took their hands, followed my senses, and teleported us to the room I sensed Vidar in. When we appeared in an office, he was sitting at his desk. He looked up, shocked.

I hesitated, and Fen rushed past me, already in wolf form. He lunged across the desk, a glorious beast too big to be as graceful as he was.

Behind us, a door slammed open, the crack of a gunshot deafened us, and Fen stumbled in mid-air with a whimper.

He landed on one knee, in human form.

"I didn't expect to see you here, Dahlia." Vidar focused on me. "You found me more quickly than I thought you would."

Why were we standing here? Why wasn't Fen attacking? I tried to summon fire, but it didn't work. Or to port us out of here, that wasn't happening either.

Panic welled inside. Fen pushed to his feet, but as he stood, black tendrils of death crept up his neck and down his arm. The wound was in a place meant to hurt like hell, but not pierce anything vital.

Magnus was keeping us shielded, protecting us though everything in the room had come to a painful stop while Vidar stared us down. But that one lapse on my part... My inability to fight the way my team needed me to, was about to cost us dearly.

And no matter how hard I focused, I couldn't get us the fuck out of here. Why did I think I could do this? Why did I trap them here?

"*Dahlia.*" Magnus was shouting my name. "Do something."

I was trying. Panic in battle wasn't my thing, no matter how much I hated the situation, but watching Fen in agony, knowing I was letting the people closest to me down—

Bragi appeared in the middle of the three of us. "To me. Now," he barked, and grabbed Fen's good arm.

Magnus and I made contact with them, too. This wasn't the time to argue.

Then we were back in NEON, in the lounge, with Fen in agony and me being fully responsible for the entire mess.

CHAPTER 17
FREYR

When Bragi vanished without a word, I'd been furious he was leaving before his betrayal was exposed.

When he reappeared seconds later with Dahlia, Magnus, and Fen in tow my relief was short lived. I recognized Fen's wound immediately—I'd seen something similar on Starkad, and I knew how difficult it was to cure.

I shoved panic and a dozen questions aside, scooped Fen in my arms, and carried him upstairs. He was too weak to do more than protest.

Everyone followed. "Call Min," I told Magnus. "Get him here now. However it needs to happen. Dahlia, ice from downstairs. Start with a large bag. We'll get more soon." I laid Fen in bed.

"How can I—"

I whirled on Bragi, grabbed his shirt, and

slammed him into the wall. All of my rage was focused into my grip. "You set us up."

"No." He shook his head. "I've been completely honest with you."

My laugh was tight and threatening. "You haven't been. You've been lying about at least one thing, your motives for being here, because I feel it. Every time you look at Magnus, I *feel* it. What else are you hiding?"

"I thought I was hiding that better. I can help you with Fen, or you can punch me, knowing when it doesn't hurt, you won't feel better."

I knew better than to hit most gods, but I also knew Bragi's weakness, and it played to my strengths. "No hitting." Letting go of his shirt, I moved my hand to his throat. There was no squeezing or choking. The skin-on-skin contact, the emotion flowing through me, would be impossible for him to ignore.

His pained gasp made me grin, but joy was one of the things I didn't currently feel.

"He saved us." Magnus was back, and her plea was timidly unlike her.

"He sent you in there. Is Min coming?" I asked.

"I can't get a hold of him. Of any of them. I'll keep trying, but please stop."

Dahlia stopped next to me and rested her hand on my arm. "Let Fen have him, once Fen's healed." Her tone was ice compared to Magnus's pleading.

And I much preferred Dahlia's logic. "Don't go anywhere." As I let go of Bragi, I intensified the barrier I kept in place to separate NEON from the rest of the world, and made sure he couldn't leave without a great deal of effort.

Dahlia sat on the edge of the bed and pressed a bag of ice to Fen's wound. I had no idea if it would help, but it didn't seem to be making things worse, so there was that.

Fen was conscious, but his face was contorted in pain.

"The bullets are made for creatures who represent death." Bragi must have a distinct wish to be fed to one, given he was still talking. "They're most effective on those who refuse to embrace their true nature. It's why they nearly killed Kirby."

I didn't want to be listening, but I couldn't help it.

"They didn't impact Dahlia at all," Magnus said.

"In some ways a dragon is the opposite of a Valkyrie—dragons are life where Valkyries are death. I don't know why Vidar thought Dahlia would be a viable target when he shot at her—maybe he hoped she had more of his blood in her," Bragi said.

Dahlia snorted. "Something to be grateful for, I suppose?"

"I'm sorry this happened to Fen. I would heal him if I could." Bragi sounded sincere.

I didn't want his apologies or sympathy or bullshit. I wanted my wolf to be all right. If Fenrir didn't make it through the next twenty-four hours, neither would Bragi.

Magnus had her phone to her ear. She would frown, pull it away long enough to jab the screen, then shove the device near her head again.

Dahlia looked like she was on the verge of tears.

Fen... it hurt to see him. The pain etched into his features ripped my heart to shreds. Had I ever felt this helpless? I needed to do something, *anything* to make sure he survived.

I pointed at Bragi. "Don't move. Don't talk. Or I will bind and gag you, and not in a fun way."

"Fuck that. You brought me here. You asked me for information, and I provided. I hope Fen lives, but you all can go fuck yourselves." Bragi vanished from the room.

I bit back a roar of frustration, but I'd hunt him down if I needed.

"Call me. Please. Please, please, please answer your phones." Magnus left the same message she'd already left several times.

I crouched next to the bed, next to Dahlia and Frey, and studied his drawn face. His eyelids fluttered, but he wasn't conscious. What could I do?

Fuck. Min and I were the same kind of god. Sex. Fertility. Life. He didn't have healing power either, but when Kirby was shot with these same bullets he'd... what? Loaned Kirby some of his life? I must be able to do the same. Focusing on that part of me was more difficult than I thought, especially with thoughts of murdering Bragi having taken up residence in my head.

I couldn't banish that desire, but I could shove it aside enough to grasp my own essence. Working carefully and quickly, I ripped open Fen's shirt and tore away the shoulder to expose his wound.

A fist clenched around my heart at the sight of the black creeping under his skin in a spiderweb of corrupted veins.

How did this work? Time to find out. I mostly ignored thoughts of torturing Bragi and mentally gripped the warmth of my core power instead.

"*Don't.*" Magnus's command wasn't enough to stop me.

I poured love and life and the promise of vengeance into the spot where my hands connected with Frey's chest.

He grunted in pain and thrashed under my touch, and agony rocketed back through me. Was it working?

"You're making him worse." Dahlia's yell penetrated my haze of hope and rage.

Magnus yanked me back, and as my physical connection was broken with Fen, I saw it—a grotesque and rotted palm mark on his chest where my hand had rested.

Fuck.

"Were you listening to Bragi?" Magnus asked.

I glared. "I was trying very hard not to."

"The magic amplifies when someone isn't accepting their association with death. Fen. You."

Creation, this was bad. I didn't dare call anyone, in this case. Most gods were in some sort of denial about who they were—the centuries had twisted us.

Was I supposed to just sit here and watch Fen suffer? I couldn't do that. Min had healed this before. Starkad had fought it in himself.

If I could let Fen accept who he was, would that help? I was almost afraid to try, but my fear had added to this. I hated to admit it, but it was true.

"Keep trying to call them." Magnus shoved her phone at Dahlia. "Frey, I know you don't want to leave, but I think I can make this right. Drop me off at the apartment. That's all I need. Drop me off and come back here. I'll handle the rest."

I stared at her blankly for a moment, forcing my brain to wrap around her words. "Okay." I took her hand, took her home, and was back by Fen's side within seconds.

This wasn't doing anyone any good, and I couldn't sit here and watch Fen fade away as I hoped that someone else might step in to fix things. "I'm going to find any immortal who might know something," I said to Dahlia. "Stay here. Call me if anything changes."

Her frown made me think she was considering arguing, but she just nodded.

Calling wouldn't work for me, because I was looking for gods who were *off the grid*. Those I hadn't talked to in decades. Centuries. Many who knew things none of us did.

I could sense a lot of the power traces I was looking for, and it wasn't a long list, but one after another told me they didn't have answers. As I moved from place to place, Bragi's information played in my mind. That a creature of death who had rejected their true nature...

If I was the reason Fen was laying at home, dying—

I had to check in on him, despite knowing Dahlia would call.

When I appeared in the bedroom, Dahlia was bent close to Fen and talking. She didn't look up. "...sorry." Her voice was soft. "This is on me, even though no one has said so. I don't know why I can't get it right. Maybe it's because I hate that I was raised to kill. I've said I'd burn the world down for Magnus, for the two of you, but I couldn't even make my dragon stick around long enough to keep you safe."

"No." Fen's croaking reply startled me. Dahlia's head shot up, and when she saw me, her cheeks turned dark pink.

I gave her a tight smile. It didn't matter what

she'd been saying, what was important was that Fen was conscious enough to speak. I gently grasped his hand.

"You don't keep me safe," Fen said. "That's my job."

She huffed and kissed his cheek. "You're an idiot. No team works well unless everyone has everyone else's back."

"We'll revisit that thought when it doesn't hurt so much." Each time Fen rasped out a word, I cringed.

Deep lines of worry were etched in Dahlia's forehead. "I wasn't done. You should've let me finish."

"No point. You're wrong." One corner of Fen's mouth twitched up.

Dahlia shook her head. "I was going to say, if you'll own this enough to get better"—she looked at me, though I suspected she was still talking to Fen—"If you'll stop fighting who you are, I'll do the same. Get better and I'll figure it out."

Deathbed bargains were never a good sign.

"Frey." Aya's voice startled me.

I turned to find her standing in the bedroom doorway, watching us with concern.

Her timing couldn't be worse. Literally. And I had no civility left, even for my own sister. "What the fuck do you want?"

CHAPTER 18

FENRIR

This was agony, and I'd had limbs ripped off that I needed to regrow. It took all of my willpower to stay conscious, not leaving me with any to shrug off the pain.

I refused to sink away in my sleep, though. I was fighting this all the way.

And I was either hallucinating, or Aya was here, and Frey wasn't happy to see her.

"I'm not here to rehash the same argument we've had too many times now."

That was actually her. The conversation might distract me a little. Neat.

"I'm here because I felt your distress," Aya said to Frey. She gasped. "What happened?"

Twins. That was right. Sometimes I forgot that they shared a deeper connection than just siblings who argued about whether or not war was coming.

Freyr and Freya were two very specific sides of the same coin, in that their powers fed, canceled, and enhanced each other's.

I tried to give Aya a wave, but didn't manage more than wiggling my fingers. My smile was probably more like a grimace.

"Fen was shot." The strain and unshed tears in Dahlia's voice squeezed my heart. I'd heard what she said, but hadn't been able to find my voice enough to assure her this wasn't her fault.

Frey explained everything we knew about the bullets, from what we'd seen with Starkad the first time we encountered them, to what Bragi told us before he left.

She offered sympathetic sounds and concerned noises at all the right parts of the story.

I was getting pretty tired of all the pity in this room. Or perhaps I was just tired.

"So Bragi implied Fen has to accept his true nature to fix this." Was that a hint of *told you so* in Aya's voice? "Why don't you just release him from this stupid oath?"

Frey clenched his fists.

I couldn't let this fall on him anymore. "He's doing it for me." *Creation* it hurt to talk.

"And he needs to stop," Aya said.

"You misunderstand." I forced each word out through gritted teeth. "He does it because I asked him to. After what happened with Astrid..." That was the first time I'd spoken that name in centuries.

She'd been a kind soul. A good person. A healer. And she was to Tyr what Frey was to me. What Dahlia was. Astrid was Tyr's anchor and a life that didn't deserve to be snuffed out when and how it was.

He'd been a brother, and when she was gone, he'd sworn I'd suffer for it.

"You've kept yourself from fighting for centuries because…" Aya sighed. "You aren't the one who killed Astrid."

"She was a casualty in *my* fight." And I wasn't convinced it hadn't been me. I was so consumed by the need to fight at the time, that I had holes in my memory. It wasn't just that I had been involved in the loss of a life like hers, but that I couldn't confirm for myself if I'd struck that killing blow.

It was that loss of control.

Aya sank into a nearby chair, and focused on me. "I need to tell you something."

"If this is some sort of deathbed confession, I'm not your priest." I tried to joke.

"*Heh.* It's not." The way Aya twisted her fingers together was unlike her. "Astrid is alive."

An intense shock gripped the wounded portion of my shoulder, feeling like someone had me in a vise. "She's not."

"Excuse me. Who's Astrid?" Dahlia asked.

"I'll introduce you sometime. You'd like her." Aya's answer wasn't enlightening.

I pushed past the fresh wave of pain. "She's my damnation."

"She was a Valkyrie," Frey said. "And she was present when Fen killed Odin."

"Just a Valkyrie?" Dahlia's voice had gone quiet. Quieter.

I tried to shake my head, but couldn't. "No. She was to Tyr what Kirby and Starkad are to each other. What Frey and I are to each other." The kind of love that spanned lifetimes. The kind that shifted and grew and changed, but didn't fade. The kind I wanted to live long enough to have with Dahlia as well.

Aya pulled her phone from her back pocket—she'd adapted to technology better than most any god, and used the internet as her main stage to monitor war. She showed me the screen. "She's back. I know where she is. She has a second chance."

I didn't know how to respond.

"You have to stop fighting who you are," Aya said. "You're not an animal, but you are denying your nature. Gods can't do that. People shouldn't either, but it kills us. Even without magic bullets, pretending we're something we're not will tear us down until we either shatter into a million pieces, or we just vanish."

"She's right." As Frey stood next to Aya, it was

clear who they each were. Both strong in their own right, neither significant to the universe with the other to counterbalance them. "I can't hold you to the oath you made. I'm releasing you."

Oh, fuck. Inspiration struck. "Do you remember when this happened to Starkad?" That was a dumb question. We'd been talking about that all night. "With Gwydion."

Frey's eyes grew wide. "Yes."

Starkad and Gwydion shared a similar bond to Frey and Aya. Drawing on that balance had... Well it hadn't healed Starkad, but it changed him. It stopped the bullet from killing him, and he was stronger for it.

"But how does that apply to you?" Dahlia asked.

I didn't have any idea.

"Perhaps the two of us can do something, where I couldn't alone." Frey looked at Aya. "Help me try?"

She held out her hand. "Of course."

If this worked, I'd—

What?

Stop fighting what I was? Swear my loyalty to some god somewhere? I'd done the latter centuries ago.

So if this worked—

I screamed when Aya and Frey pressed interlocked hands to my shoulder and filled me with the sensation of having my arm ripped off and simultaneously crammed into my body. They jerked away immediately. My breath came in jagged gasps. *Holy fuck* that hurt. "Did it do anything?" I wanted the pain to be worth it.

Frey furrowed his brow. "It looked like it was going to, but then it stopped."

That explained the *push and pull* feeling. But there was something to this theory; there had to be. "Dahlia needs to try."

"I...What?" She dropped my hand and stared at me in shock.

Maybe delirium was setting in, but it made as much sense as anything. "Bragi said dragons were life."

"He's got a good point," Frey said.

Dahlia worried her bottom lip and looked between us. "But Frey already tried. Why would I be different?"

"Because you *are* different." In this state of mind, it was obvious to me. The reason I'd made space for her in my heart, why Frey and I kept her in our lives, was that she was unlike anyone I'd known throughout history. Did that mean she could heal whatever this was? Maybe not. But it seemed like the odds were better.

"All right. Here goes nothing." She laid her hand over my wound.

Nothing happened.

She sighed and pulled away. "See? I've been touching you all night and nothing's changed."

"Try again. Try harder." I wouldn't be conscious much longer. Darkness licked the edges of my vision.

"I *am*. Do you think I want this to happen to you?" Dahlia's voice inched up in volume. "I don't want you to suffer. I don't want you lying here. I don't want to go through eternity knowing that Vidar won at anything—especially *this*. If I could reach inside you and rip out the infection right now, if I could make myself, you, all of us, accept our places in this world, I'd be doing exactly that."

The pain in her words was tangible, mingling with my own. "Because the thing I want more than anything, the thing I've always wanted, is to belong." Dahlia's voice cracked. "And I finally do. With Magnus. With the two of you. When I'm with you, I feel like I actually belong in this world. Like I know where I fit. If I'm a dragon. A killer. A goofy girl who hides behind way too many Star Wars refer-ences, it doesn't matter, because I belong with you, and if you're gone, I won't have a place anymore. And maybe that's selfish, and maybe that's why I can't help you, but gods damn it, *I'm trying*." She was shouting when she finished, and wet tracks traced down her cheeks.

So much passion. Raw and powerful. She had that in common with Frey. I did so adore Dahlia.

I grasped Frey's hand with my good one. "Who I am doesn't bother me the way it used to." As I said the words, they felt true. It hadn't been a problem for a while, but I'd become so used to fighting it. "I'm a fucking god of war." Raising my injured arm hurt in a way nothing ever had, but I pushed through the pain. "And I will battle anyone who dares threaten either of you. That doesn't mean death is all there is. I need you both here." I grasped Dahlia's hand as well. "Regardless of whether or not you believe in yourself," I looked her in the eye. "I do."

I pulled both of their hands to my chest, until their knuckles met. Until the three of us were connected.

Sparks shot up from the touch and heat seared my skin where it met theirs. The pain in my shoulder was as if someone had reached a hand into my bullet wound and was yanking out my heart.

I gripped their hands tight through my roar of pain, not wanting to let go of either Frey or Dahlia.

And then the agony was gone. Completely.

I collapsed back on the bed with a grunt. I should be exhausted, but the energy that coursed through me was better than in a long time. I felt cleansed.

"Fuck me." Frey collapsed with his head on my chest. "Tell me that worked."

"It worked." I flexed my previously-bad hand as much as I could without letting go of Dahlia. I tugged her in next to us and held both her and Frey tight.

Aya lingered in the background, looking uncomfortable. She sighed. "Well, I'm going to go, now that the distress is gone." She waved.

"I want to meet Astrid. To see her again," I said.

Aya nodded. "When she's ready. For now, the three of you need some alone time." With that, she vanished.

I could lay like this for hours. Days. Weeks.. Just wrapped up in Frey and Dahlia.

She stiffened under my touch, then bolted straight up. Her face was pinched and her eyes glazed over. "Magnus?"

CHAPTER 19
DAHLIA

I knew now what I'd seen in my vision. The one I had in Perth. It looked wrong, it felt wrong, because I saw it all through my eyes.

And now I was stuck in it again, with fire and pain and a broken heart that all made my gut churn.

At the center of it all was Magnus, and I watched again and again as Vidar slaughtered her.

"Dahlia."

Was she screaming my name?

No. That was Fen. He was with me, fighting by my side. I could see him now.

"*Dahlia.*" This time his voice was more insistent.

That wasn't coming from in my head or the fight. It *was* next to me though. I clawed my way out of the vision to find Fen and Frey watching me with concern.

While I adored them for their concern, I was

getting real fucking tired of coming to and finding those *what's wrong with Dahlia now* expressions.

It didn't matter. "I need to go. Now." I wasn't sure how I knew, but I was certain that vision was about to happen.

"Whoa." Frey grabbed my wrist as I stood. "You just finished a horrific fight and then an emotional battle after. You haven't slept. You know better than to run into a situation unprepared."

I did, but this was different. "There's no time for prep. Magnus is confronting Vidar. *Now*. I don't have the luxury of anything but backing her up." This was taking too much time. Did I need better clothes? A firearm? It didn't matter. I was going in there as a dragon, and making sure she stayed alive.

Fen was already on his feet. "Okay. We're going with you."

"You just healed." I couldn't lose him again, either.

"Like you said, that doesn't matter. I'm fine. Let's go. Are you coming with us?" He looked at Frey.

Frey nodded. "Where?"

I couldn't explain, but I felt it. I could picture it as surely as I could our apartment. My growing panic and sense of impending doom was impossible to ignore. If I didn't act now, I'd crawl out of my skin. I grabbed both their hands and let the vision and my instinct take us to a new location.

To most people the room we appeared in might

look like a giant concrete cave, but I recognized it as a TOM indoor combat facility. Obstacles could be moved in for urban warfare training or hand to hand combat. Right now it was wide open, making it look vast.

"*Incoming.*" At Magnus's shout, Fen, Frey, and I dove in different directions.

A large fireball hit the ground where we'd been standing, peppering us with chunks of rock.

"He's all healed. I'd love to know how you did that." Vidar's voice seemed to come from everywhere.

Magnus in her full Valkyrie form landed next to us. "Shield." Which meant she was currently protecting us.

That didn't mean we could afford to stay stationary or catch up. "Glad you're alive," I said.

"Same. All of you." She looked Fen over. "He's stronger than you realize."

"Yeah, he is." Fen's voice came from inside our heads, as he'd become a large wolf.

"All for you, Fenrir." It wasn't like Vidar's vice was echoing or coming from speakers. He sounded like he personally was speaking from multiple points in the room.

There weren't any real spots to hide, so I extended my focus to pick out the hotspots of his power, and try to eliminate which weren't him.

I wasn't there yet, but I had a good idea. "Fen.

North. Fifty meters. Magnus, south south west seventy-five. I'm going east. Frey, if it moves, pin it down."

We all broke into our separate directions.

It should be an easy fight, four against one, with one of us having centuries of experience, one of us having the ability to put up a magical shield, and me.

Attacks rained in on us from random directions, pelting Magnus's shield, and occasionally getting through. With our attentions divided, we could head toward each Vidar apparition, but with his ability to vanish and appear in a blink, it didn't matter.

I struggled to anticipate his every move, teleporting to follow him, but it wasn't working, and Frey wasn't having any more success than I did.

Within minutes, it was clear that the four of us were exhausted, and Vidar didn't show any sign of slowing down.

A ball of flame slammed into Magnus's chest, knocking her onto her back. She wasn't moving.

My vision, the prophecy that had played out in my mind, overlapped with reality, and I was already flying toward her. Another fireball knocked me back, and then a series of more, making me stutter in my trip, but not stopping me.

A giant spear of light appeared in the air, sliced through the room, and buried itself in Magnus's chest, pinning her to the ground.

No. "I need help," I shouted, and Fen was instantly by my side as I raced to Magnus.

Frey's magic wasn't doing a great job of pinning Vidar down, because most of his attacks weren't coming from him or from his movement.

I reached Magnus's side, where she lay unmoving.

Frey put up a shield around us.

Hundreds of tiny shards of flame appeared inside, pelting us all, slicing through our skin and leaving ugly streaks of dark red as the onslaught of tiny cuts appeared and healed.

Except Magnus wasn't healing.

My fear spiked. I pressed my fingers to her throat, looking for a pulse.

The longer she lay there, the more damage she took.

I shook her. Needing her to be okay.

"She's gone." Frey's muttered words were full of disbelief.

"No." I didn't believe it, even though I no longer felt her. "She's not. She can't be."

"It's true." Vidar's taunting dug into my thoughts and heart. "Bye-bye, Magnus."

Rage replaced my disbelief, and a whole new power screamed through my veins. I felt everything about me that was a dragon. I saw flame in my mind, and it appeared in spirals around my arms. Flinging it at every point of attack at once was instinct.

I was in full control of my power. I blinked into sight and out again, working to keep Vidar on his toes rather than trying to anticipate his moves. Each time I appeared, I registered his location, attacked, and moved again. My goal was to hit him so fast he couldn't recover.

A trick I'd learned from watching him.

Fen matched my pace, though he was leaping rather than teleporting. He hit Vidar when I pulled back. We had him off-guard.

Magnus was gone.

The thought echoed in my mind as I lit into Vidar with unrelenting rage.

She was dead.

It couldn't be true.

But I could see her body from here. Unmoving. She had no magical signature. She didn't give off any spark of life.

I appeared in a new spot as Fen leaped to the same point, and we both stumbled. We corrected course within a heartbeat.

The mistake gave Vidar enough time to snap his fingers.

Magnus's body vanished in a ball of flame. Like that, she was nothing more than an ashen shadow on the blood-stained concrete.

Something echoed off the concrete walls. It was my scream.

I wasn't lost in the dragon. I knew exactly what I

was doing. I summoned every bit of power, from every corner of my mind, body, and the universe, that I could reach, and wrapped Vidar in a ball of flame.

His shout of agony didn't alleviate my pain, but I didn't stop until he was gone. Obliterated.

I couldn't feel him anywhere in the world. Vidar was dead.

But so was Magnus.

I sank to the concrete, not caring that it bit into my knees or that I was human again. She was gone.

I was vaguely aware of someone touching me. I didn't have the strength to shrug Frey off.

"We need to go," Fen said.

I traced my fingers above the Magnus-shadow on the ground, not making contact. Not trusting myself to speak or even think.

"I'm sorry." Frey sounded like he meant it.

Of course he did, but it didn't matter. *Sorry* wouldn't bring back my sister.

The concrete bunker vanished, and we were back in the apartment. I wanted to scream *take me back*, but what was the point?

She was gone. Like that.

Every member of the TOM board was about to suffer at my hand, in her name. It might not bring her back, but fuck those guys.

CHAPTER 20
FREYR

It had taken some strong magic to make sure Dahlia went to sleep. Not that I blamed her for her reaction, but she needed rest. Vengeance worked better when the mind was at its best, and I wouldn't stop her from what I suspected she was planning.

It wrenched my heart to watch Fen watch Dahlia as she slept. So many thoughts raced through my mind. So many emotions in my heart. I couldn't begin to name them.

"What now?" I asked softly, letting my unspoken *besides the obvious* hang between us.

Fen raked his fingers through his hair. "She found it."

"Found...?" I knew the answer. I needed to hear it anyway.

"Her dragon. She embraced it." He was stating the obvious rather than answering my question.

But I didn't blame him either. "The price we paid tonight was too high for this."

Fen let out a shaky sigh, with a hint of whimper in it. "It was. And there's no going back. On anything. She's a part of me now—Dahlia is—as much as you are. There's also no taking back how much I love her."

After what happened to heal him, and even what came before now, the words didn't surprise me, and there was no jealousy. If he had enough love for both of us, I could accept that. "I know, and I don't suspect I'm that far off." I loved Dahlia too, and while I wasn't sure I could give her the eternal promise of my heart yet, if things kept going down this path, it wouldn't be long until I did. "But this could break her."

"No." Fen clenched his jaw. "This will leave deep scars, but she won't wilt. She realizes now who she is. I just wish..."

That we hadn't lost Magnus in the process. That it didn't have to hurt Dahlia so much. I tangled my fingers with his and squeezed. "I do too."

CHAPTER 21

FENRIR

Despite being magically induced, Dahlia's sleep was anything but magical. She spent most of the time whimpering, tossing, and turning.

I stayed next to her, hoping my being nearby would reach some part of her and offer comfort, even in her unconsciousness. As the centuries passed, she'd lose more and more people she cared about, but knowing that wouldn't help her now.

Besides, she'd learn to distance herself from more and more people. I didn't look forward to that. The notion that immortality would make her cynical turned my stomach. And Magnus wasn't just anyone.

When she woke, silent tears streaming down her face and sobs wracking her body, I pulled her into my arms and let her cry until she was spent.

"Come on." I placed her on her feet.

"Why?"

"Because I said so." I led her into the bathroom and sat her on the closed toilet seat. When the water running in the sink was a good temperature, I wetted a washcloth, knelt in front of her, and cleaned her face. "Shower later." I sniffed the air. "Frey's making breakfast." He must've heard us moving around.

"It's the middle of the afternoon."

I drew a thumb over her cheek, marveling at how soft and fragile she was, even now that she was immortal. "Since when does time of day matter when it comes to eating breakfast?"

"Since never. Is she really gone?"

My heart fractured at the forlorn crack in Dahlia's voice. "Yes. I'm sorry."

She sniffled and her chin quivered. She drew in a shuddering breath. "We were supposed to grow old together."

Now seemed like a bad time to point out they weren't going to grow old anyway. Instead, I settled for taking Dahlia's hands between mine.

"I understand that it's not the same." I leaned in and pressed my forehead to hers. "But I'm hoping you'll grow old with me. With us. I do love you. In a different way but just as much as I love Frey, and I'm here for you. So is he."

She leaned more weight against me, and a splash

of wetness struck the back of my hand. Tears were sliding down her cheeks again.

"Take as much time as you need," I said. "Today, and going forward. I'm here to be whatever you need."

She pulled one hand away to drag the back of her wrist across her face. The gesture didn't so much dry her skin as spread the misery. "I need Magnus back."

The one thing I couldn't do.

"But I love you too," Dahlia said softly. "Thank you for being here."

"Always." At least I could promise that.

When the pain had numbed a little, in a few weeks or a few months, or however long it took, I'd warn her and Frey about the scent in the air. It was similar to moisture right before a storm, but this wasn't rain, it was death.

The beginning of the end was here. Death meant rebirth, but like now, it also meant pain.

I'd do everything in my power to shield her from this kind of pain again.

CHAPTER 22
DAHLIA

I stood at the edge of a grove of trees at the foot of Mount Yoshino in Japan. This was one of Magnus's favorite places.

"Now you can watch the trees bloom every year." I set a claw-shaped, full-fingered ring at the base of one of the trees, and tucked into a spot where no one would find it but me. Or her. The jewelry was carved from one of my own claws—a replica of one I'd purchased for her a few years back. The original had been made from Artura's claw and defiled by blood magic that Vidar used to make it powerful.

This one was all me. Imbued with a hint of dragon power and heavy doses of how desperately I missed her.

It had been a couple of weeks, and I still struggled not to cry when I thought about Magnus. There were days when I wanted to curl up in a ball and never move again.

Frey suggested this might help me say *goodbye.* He and Fen stood a few feet back, watching. Waiting. They'd been so gloriously patient with me. I wanted to stop hurting, just so they could stop worrying, but I didn't know how.

"I'm really good at summoning my dragon now," I said to spot where I would've scattered Magnus's ashes if I had any to scatter. "I hate that I can do some of these things because of him, but I'm going to use it to tear down TOM. I'll destroy every last piece of the empire he helped build."

I expected an argument to come from behind me, though neither Fen nor Frey had done anything to dissuade the research I'd been doing over the past few weeks. "Fen says I should go full dragon and burn everything down. I don't think I'd make a good Targaryen, and I don't want any of the soldiers to suffer. But the gods. The board..."

My plan was coming together nicely. I was using my power, both digital and magical, to follow the tracks of every TOM founder. I was still missing a name or two from my list, but I'd figure out who they were soon enough.

This wouldn't be a strictly physical war. They'd integrated themselves with this world, and that meant digital destruction. "Kirby promised to help me. And Brit. Starkad. No surprise there. But Fen has some connections who are going to help, too. Same for Aya and even Artura. I know it won't bring you back, and I have no idea where Valkyries go when they die, but if you can see me from whatever afterlife you're in, I'd much rather you were here."

If I said much more, I'd start to bawl again, and my eyes couldn't take any more of that today. Instant healing didn't seem to mean shit when it came to trauma.

I tucked away the ring, collected myself, and turned to Fen and Frey. "I need to make one more stop," I said. "I'll meet you back at NEON?"

Frey squeezed my hand and kissed me on the cheek.

Fen pressed his lips to mine. "Be safe," he murmured against my skin.

I nodded and vanished. The instant I reappeared in the apartment I'd shared with Magnus, an intense weight pressed in on my chest, threatening to suffocate me.

We didn't have much stuff, so there wasn't much packing to do, but I couldn't today. This had been ours, and now it was another broken promise about our future.

I wouldn't be back here anytime soon, either. I wrapped the entire place in a dragon spell, tying the magic to the walls of the apartment, so I wouldn't need to hold onto it. Now the door would still sit in the mortal world, but the apartment itself would rest in another plane. One where time passed more slowly.

"Your death won't be in vain," I said to the empty room, mostly to try to convince myself. At least I could keep one promise—I'd burn it all down to avenge my sister.

IF YOU CAN'T BELIEVE I'd end the book there, make sure you check out SABOTAGE (NEON BOOK 3), for more twisty, turny, spicy gods, shifters, and the women they love.